A STAR REPORTER IS MISSING!

Ronald Wilford, cub reporter on the *Cleveland Star*, is asked by his editor to find a missing colleague and friend, Barry Knight, and discover why he disappeared. Knight, who pulls no punches when he writes, has many enemies among the local racketeers and shady politicians he has exposed. Ronald, with the help of his younger brother Ted (hero of *The Locked Safe Mystery*), uncovers a strange and fascinating puzzle.

An unusual ending to this absorbing mystery is provided when Ronald is faced with an interesting ethical problem, both as a reporter and a friend, which he must solve in order to wind up the case.

THE STAR REPORTER MYSTERY

TED WILFORD MYSTERY SERIES

NORVIN PALLAS

WILDSIDE PRESS

ACKNOWLEDGMENTS

The Wildside Press reprints of the Ted Wilford series were made possible by the assistance of many people, including Norvin Pallas's family; Steve Romberger, whose copy of *The Secret of Thunder Mountain* was ultimately used to create this edition; George Beatty and James D. Keeline, who provided copies of many of the texts and covers; and David M. Baumann, whose essay "A Dark Horse Series" was an invaluable reference for reprinting the stories; and of course Wildside's production team, Shawn Garrett, Helen McGee, Sam Hogan, and Steve Coupe.

To my mother

Published by Wildside Press LLC.
www.wildsidepress.com

CHAPTER 1

Barry Knight Is Missing

It was nearly eight o'clock, on the second morning after Christmas, when Ronald Wilford came up the steps of the Cleveland Union Terminal, carrying a suitcase. He had had an enjoyable vacation at home in the little town of Forestdale, spending Christmas with his mother, his younger brother Ted, and some family friends. He had revisited the office of the *Town Crier,* the local newspaper where he had made his start, and where his outstanding work had enabled him to get a job on a metropolitan daily.

But it was pleasant to be getting back to his job again, too. The smell of fresh newsprint and printer's ink, the rolling of the great rotary presses, the hustle of the newspaper office—all had an elusive attraction that he missed when he was away too long.

He had taken the sleeper in, which allowed him an extra day at home, but he hadn't eaten on the train—not at Pullman prices, not without an expense account. Glancing at the big terminal clock, he decided he'd just have time for a little snack at the coffee shop off the main lobby, below street level, before reporting to the office.

Stopping only long enough to pick up a morning paper from the newsstand, he entered the shop and found a seat on a stool in front of the counter.

"Hi, Ronald," the waitress greeted him.

"Hello, Sandra. Anything new in town while I was gone?"

"Nothing much. Judging by the *Twilight Star,* the whole town's in hibernation. They must have given the entire staff a vacation. You should have seen the big banner headline Christmas morning: *'SANTA CLAUS ARRIVES ON SCHEDULE.'* Kind of corny for a big city, but I guess people liked it."

"The Fire Chief goes for those sentimental touches once in a while."

The editor of the *Star,* Jason Burnett, had acquired his nickname as a young reporter when, it was alleged, he generally managed to beat the fire engines to the scene of a fire. Maybe it never happened more than once or twice, and only then by accident, but a reputation like that didn't hurt anything in the newspaper business.

Ronald gave the menu only the briefest glance, before deciding, "Bacon and scrambled eggs, orange juice, coffee, and toast, please."

"Coming up!"

Sandra had been very nearly right, Ronald concluded, as he looked over the front page while waiting for his breakfast. All the big stories had come in on the wire. There seemed to be very little of purely local interest, other than a few accidents. Fortunately no big disaster had marred the holiday scene. Elections were all out of the way, sports were in the doldrums, and if there were any big exposés coming up, the editors were sitting on them until after the first of the year. This was the usual post-Christmas slump.

Coming out of the terminal, Ronald saw that this was to be a clear, cold day. The city must have had plenty of snow, but the snow removal crews had been efficient, at least on the principal arteries. Loads of salt had turned the snow into slush, and trucks had hauled most of it away, although here and there were huge piles awaiting attention. The Christmas tree still stood on the square, which was no novelty to Ronald, for it had been erected immediately after Thanksgiving, though it retained a fresh, sparkling look. Even the soldiers' and sailors' monument, which many people condemned as an artistic monstrosity and civic eyesore, conveyed a "welcome home" feeling.

Because he still had a few minutes to spare, Ronald decided against fighting the winds across the square, and turned up Euclid Avenue instead. Then he crossed Euclid and entered the arcade, where he climbed the stairs to the Superior Avenue level. A small matter was weighing on his mind, and he kept turning it over and over again.

Would it be all right for a raw cub reporter like himself to ask Barry Knight, the paper's hard-hitting crime reporter, to have lunch with him? Well, why not? he argued. They had worked on several assignments together. Knight had given him a helping hand during his early difficult days on the paper, even covered up a couple of his blunders. Just the same, Knight was a person who was a little difficult to approach. His uncompromising newspaper stories had earned him many enemies, and although he knew a great many people, there was no one who could accurately be described as his friend. Something about Knight repelled gestures of friendship.

Still, somebody's got to take the first step, Ronald decided. His growing experience with the many people he had met had taught him that most people are friendly, if you can only get them to thaw out. Why shouldn't the same be true of Knight? Anyway, it was only a lunch. By the time he had crossed Superior Avenue he had made up his mind to ask him.

Passing the large windows through which the printing presses could be seen, he headed upstairs toward the editorial rooms. Because of the reputation Knight had earned for himself, he rated a private office and secretary, and Ronald saw that Miss Curtis was already at work. He stuck his head in the door.

"Hello, Miss Curtis. Has Knight been in yet?"

"Not yet, Ronald."

Ronald never felt quite at ease with Miss Curtis. Although friendly enough in the office, a couple of times she had passed him on the street and had cut him off with the coolest glance. Apparently she was determined that their relationship should be strictly a business one, and if that was the way she wanted it, Ronald was content to leave it that way for the present.

He stepped into the office and hesitated. "Do you happen to know, Miss Curtis, whether Knight has any plans for lunch today?"

"I don't know, Ronald. Knight hasn't been in for several days. I haven't seen him since the day you left."

"You haven't?" Ronald frowned. "I didn't know he was going to take off."

"No, I didn't either." And now Ronald noticed that she looked very worried.

"Hasn't he called in?"

"No."

"That doesn't sound like Knight. Did you try to phone him?"

"Five times yesterday, and twice this morning. There wasn't any answer. I don't know—holidays always sort of depressed Knight—I suppose it's not having any family, or anything. Anyway I wasn't too much worried until this morning." She remembered something then. "Oh, Ronald, Burnett wants to see you in his office right away."

"The Fire Chief himself? Well, what do you know?"

"I think he's waiting for you. I'm pretty sure it has something to do with Knight."

The editor's door was open, and Ronald walked in.

"You wanted to see me, Burnett?"

As a newcomer, Ronald had always addressed the editor as Mr. Burnett, until one day his superior had called him in and told him they didn't have time for titles on a newspaper. Later Ronald learned that this was a standard speech, which informed a cub that he had passed his trial and was now accepted as a permanent member of the staff. Office boys and new cubs, though, still called the editor "Mr. Burnett."

"Yes, Wilford. I won't ask you to sit down because it'll only take a moment. I don't know what's happened to Knight, and I want you to run out to his home and find out. It may be that the big goof is sick and ashamed to admit it. Anyway, we'll try to pretend that's all it is until we learn something different."

"Right. I'll check in at the city desk—"

"Don't bother. I've talked to Fogarty already. And when you get back, report directly to me. I'm very much interested—or maybe worried would be a better word. Just put that suitcase down somewhere—it doesn't have a bomb in it, I suppose?"

"I don't know. I hope you find out before I do."

Leaving the building, Ronald turned northward toward the lake and walked rapidly to the parking lot where he had left his car before the Christmas holiday. He had expected that he might have to dig it out of the snow, but fortunately it was parked to the leeward side of one of the tall buildings, and there was no trouble. His battery, too, proved equal to the occasion. Within a few minutes he was on his way across the valley over the Main Avenue Bridge. There was a cloverleaf at the western approach to the bridge, and he recalled that the first time he had tried to negotiate it he had been—well, if not lost, at least temporarily confused.

But he no longer had any trouble there and easily made the turn into the lake-shore drive. Traffic eastward was still heavy, but in his direction there was little congestion, and he drove as rapidly as winter conditions would permit. To his right, off Edgewater Park, was Lake Erie, and he could see that the water was frozen, far out past the breakwater, in the rough fashion typical of a large, restless body of water. All shipping had ceased nearly two months before.

When he was far enough west, he turned south until he reached Franklin Boulevard. Although he had Knight's number, he had never visited him at home before. Knight didn't encourage that type of intimacy, although Ronald was perhaps as close to him as anyone. When he had found the right number, it proved to be a fine old home that had since degenerated into a rooming house. Ronald's ring was answered by the landlady, who asked him inside and introduced herself as Mrs. Patrunik.

"I'm from the *Star*, Mrs. Patrunik. Knight hasn't reported in for several days, and we're wondering what happened to him."

"I wish I knew that myself. His phone was ringing all day yesterday, and I wanted to answer, but his door was locked. Of course I have another key, but I didn't feel—"

"Quite right, Mrs. Patrunik. Then I take it he isn't here?"

"Oh, yes, he's not here. He left the Thursday morning before Christmas. I heard him leave the house about the usual time, and so I supposed he'd merely gone to work. But later I found his suitcase was missing—"

She stopped quickly, and Ronald smiled to himself. She *had* used her key after all.

"He didn't check out, then? The room's still paid for in advance?"

"Certainly, I've never had any trouble like that with Mr. Knight. With some of my roomers, perhaps, but Mr. Knight is a gentleman of high character."

"I'm well aware of that, Mrs. Patrunik. Then you have no idea at all where he went or when he'll be back?"

"No, I do not. Of course it was Christmas time, and so many people were going home, but I understood he didn't have any family. Christmas is such a dreary time to be alone. I had thought perhaps I might be able to bring a little cheer into his holiday, but he didn't stay."

Ronald considered. "Would it be all right for me to see his room, Mrs. Patrunik?"

"You didn't have in mind going through his papers and things like that, did you?"

"No, nothing like that," Ronald assured her, but did not explain further. To himself, he wondered just what he expected to find that would be of any help to him. If Knight had taken himself off voluntarily, as seemed to be the case, there wouldn't be any clues left lying around the room.

Mrs. Patrunik was saying, "I hope you won't mind showing me your credentials, young man? I've no doubt you're who you say you are, but Mr. Knight knew a great many people, not all of the best sort. A man of high character himself, but I can't say as much for some of his acquaintances."

Mechanically, Ronald produced his press card. Apparently satisfied, Mrs. Patrunik led the way upstairs and unlocked a bedroom door. Ronald stepped into the room, with the landlady close behind him. It was a large combination bedroom and sitting room, with a huge old-fashioned bedstead, a bureau, a table and several matching chairs, a large easy chair and a reading lamp in front of a bookcase, a desk with a telephone, and a radio-television-phonograph set. The contents of the desk drawers might have been enlightening, but he knew Mrs. Patrunik wouldn't allow him to take such a liberty, and he doubted whether he could find anything of immediate value in any case. Instead he turned his attention to the clothes closet.

Walking across the room he threw open the door. "I hope you don't mind," he said, but although Mrs. Patrunik did not answer, she had followed him and was watching him very closely. Ronald looked through the clothes on the hangers. It appeared to him that only summer clothes remained, and that Knight had taken all his winter things with him. The suitcase, too, if there really had been one, was missing. He did discover one thing that surprised him, a violin case on the shelf.

"Is that Knight's?" he asked. "I didn't know he was a musician."

"I've never heard him play," the landlady replied. "I dusted it off once in a while, but I don't think he ever opened it himself."

But a trained musician treasures his instrument and plays on it regularly, which keeps it in trim and enhances its value, Ronald thought. Still, he had no assurance that it was a valuable instrument, after all, or that Knight was even able to play it.

That seemed to be all the room had to offer, and Ronald went downstairs, though with a feeling of reluctance. After thanking Mrs. Patrunik, and having her promise to call the newspaper if anything should turn up, he left the building.

He returned downtown by way of Franklin. This had once been a tree-lined boulevard, but now many of the big trees were gone. He recalled that a tornado had struck this area several years before. First sighted near the airport, the tornado's cone had dipped near West 117th Street, wiping out a new real-estate development, then had cut a swath through the West Side, uprooting most of the tree population, before dipping once more near Franklin and Twenty-fifth with disastrous results. Then it had swept across the valley, still gusty enough to blow out a charity street fair on Short Vincent—for once the Vincent Street know-it-alls had been caught short themselves—before losing itself over the lake. This was the story that had brought Knight into prominence with his on-the-spot reporting, though a worse tornado the same day in Flint, and one the next day in Worcester, had deprived him of national attention.

Approaching Twenty-fifth at Rowdy Row, he decided that as long as he was out this way he might as well stop at the Daisy Avenue police precinct. Most of Knight's important tips came through the central station, but there were times when he thought he could do more on the precinct level, and this was one of his haunts.

Ronald knew the officer at the desk, Sergeant Hensel, and he tried to make his voice sound casual.

"Thought I'd look in and see if you had anything for me."

"Look over the blotter if you want to," Hensel replied carelessly. But there were going to be questions just the same, for why was a cub reporter cutting in on Knight's territory, if Knight were available? "What's happened to Knight? I haven't seen him since last Thursday."

"Wednesday," said the patrolman at his elbow. "I remember, because I had peanut butter sandwiches in my lunch."

"His wife always puts peanut butter sandwiches in his lunch," the sergeant remarked to Ronald. "It was Thursday."

Ronald made a pretense of looking over the blotter; there was nothing there that the regular police reporter couldn't just as well pick up later. "Did he say what he wanted?"

But the sergeant wasn't at all deceived by Ronald's manner. "What's the matter? Did you lose him, or something?"

"Not exactly, only he hasn't yet returned from his holiday. Did he want anything in particular when you saw him last Thursday?"

"Said he was looking for a character named Dixie Orlando, which is just odd enough that it might be his real name."

The bars were down now, and Ronald knew that they weren't fooling each other. "Do you know where I can find this Orlando fellow?"

Hensel raised his hands hopelessly. "Where do you ever find a Short Vincent character except on Vincent Street? That's all I know."

Without explaining further, Ronald thanked him and left. He didn't feel he had accomplished a great deal, except that now he knew for sure that Barry Knight was missing, had left suddenly and without explanation, with no known motive, and that maybe some character named Dixie Orlando might know something about it.

CHAPTER 2

Short Vincent

Returning to the office, Ronald reported directly to Burnett.

"Well, what did you find out, Wilford?" Burnett asked him.

"He's gone, all right. As nearly as I can make out, he packed up his winter clothes and left without saying anything to anybody. The only clue I picked up was that he'd been asking at the precinct station for a Vincent Street character named Dixie Orlando. Does the name mean anything to you?"

"Orlando? Yes, I've heard it before. I think Miss Curtis would know more about that than I do." The editor paced briskly back and forth, one time knocking into Ronald's suitcase. Ronald made a movement to pick it up, but Burnett stopped him with a wave of the hand. "Don't bother. That's only the third time this morning. We're old friends by now."

His face was very thoughtful, and at last he said, "I don't mind admitting that I'm very much worried about this, Wilford. I want you to drop everything else and stick with it. We'll transfer Corrigan to police court—he'll be glad to get off crank calls. All you've got to worry about is finding Knight! I won't say don't come back without him, but be sure you come back with something."

"Wilco!"

"I guess you know what's biting me. Knight's type of reporting has won him a lot of enemies, and I want to be sure they haven't had anything to do with this."

"Well, O.K.," said Ronald, a little doubtfully.

"What's on your mind, Wilford?"

"It's just that I can't imagine Knight running away from trouble. He isn't that kind. And it certainly looks to me as though he left voluntarily."

"Unless he was threatened."

"That's just it. I don't think Knight would give in to threats."

"Look at it another way, Wilford. He isn't the kind who would just go off without letting us know, either. He doesn't always tell what kind of investigation he's working on, but he usually tells how long he's going to be gone and where we can reach him. If he isn't working on a case, and he hasn't left because of threats, what's he up to, anyway?"

"I'll get right at it," Ronald agreed, as the editor finally stopped pacing and sat down at the desk. "Any ideas where it might be best to start? How about my trying to locate this Dixie Orlando on Short Vincent?"

"Wilford," said Burnett patiently, "in many ways I'm a hardhearted man, but I don't believe in throwing a lamb to the wolves. Now don't get sore about my calling you a lamb. It's only that you're new to the city and aren't ready for Short Vincent yet. A reporter can't get along in this city without knowing Short Vincent, but there'll be plenty of time later for you. Ask Miss Curtis to let you see Knight's story about it sometime. There'd be a good place to start, Wilford—with Miss Curtis. She knows more about Knight's affairs than I do. Work along with her, use your expense account liberally if necessary, and give me progress reports from time to time—but stay away from Short Vincent! When those guys put two and two together, they generally come up with six."

Ronald found Miss Curtis at her desk, which was buried under the weight of Knight's correspondence, a job she was trying to handle in his absence.

"Is it always this bad?" he asked her.

"Oh, no, it all depends. Sometimes it slackens down to only twenty or thirty letters a day. But just after Knight has published one of his exposé series of articles, the tide seems to come rolling in."

"What's this tide from? Knight hasn't done anything like that for the last couple of weeks."

"No, this is about the last sweep from that series he did on the slot-machine racket. I imagine it's about over by now. People get all stirred up for a while, but they won't do anything very constructive about it, and soon it all blows over and things are back operating just about the way they were before." She sighed.

Accustomed though he was to sitting on the edges of desks, which seemed to provide just about the proper amount of stretch for his long legs, Ronald decided there wasn't room this time, and he pulled over a chair instead.

"Miss Curtis, Burnett wants you to work with me on this Knight affair—doesn't want me to stop until I find him."

"That sounds logical," she decided, turning from the correspondence with a hopeless air and facing Ronald. "I'd say I'm pretty deeply in it already."

"Now the question is where to begin. Did you ever hear of a man named Dixie Orlando?"

She studied him for a moment. "What do you know about Orlando?"

"Knight was asking for him just before he disappeared."

She considered the matter. "I really didn't want to say anything, Ronald, but I suppose it's best. Dixie Orlando was one of Knight's Short Vincent informants. I don't know too much about what went on—this was one of the things that Knight covered up from me. But I have reason to believe he often acted as Knight's leg man for out-of-town assignments. I wasn't supposed to know about this. Often letters would come in, in a certain style of handwriting. They were marked personal, so I never opened them. And there was never any return address. But you know how hard it is to keep a secret like that from a secretary. A letter would come in, and I would lay it aside for Knight. Sometime afterward he would remark something about Dixie Orlando. Of course it didn't take me long to put things together and figure out that these letters came from Orlando."

"Where were they postmarked?"

"A good many of them came from the state capital—not always, though."

"What do you know about Orlando? Is he the criminal type?"

"I—I really couldn't say about that. Don't misunderstand me. Knight wouldn't consort with questionable characters, not even for the sake of a story. But he had a peculiar philosophy. He said that you have to judge a man by what he is now—not by what he used to be. This might have applied to Orlando."

"Supposing that Orlando did have a doubtful past, isn't it possible he might have turned criminal again? Could he have become violent, threatened Knight, anything like that?"

"I don't think so, Ronald. I never met him personally, but from the things Knight said about him—no, I don't believe anything like that could have happened."

Ronald meditated. "Just the same I'd like to know what it was Knight wanted to see Orlando about. I wanted to go down to Short Vincent and inquire about him, but Burnett said no."

"Burnett's right," Miss Curtis assured him. "That's not the way you do things on Short Vincent. Even Knight, you observed, didn't do that. Why, if you really had anything on him, you might scare him all the way to California before you could put your finger on him."

"Haven't you ever been down to Short Vincent?" he asked curiously.

"For lunch, yes—but not as a reporter. That's why it's more important for you to watch your step."

"Then what do I do?"

"As far as Short Vincent is concerned, you don't do anything at all. You wait for Short Vincent to come to you."

The situation could hardly have been more puzzling to Ronald, but he knew by now that there are angles to big-city reporting that aren't found in a small town. Miss Curtis must be right, for Burnett had warned him about Short Vincent, too. He leaned back in the swivel chair.

"Then as long as Short Vincent seems to be out for the moment, I can only think of two other approaches. One is to find out all I can about Barry Knight. The other is to find out all I can about his possible enemies."

"You might find both of those pretty tall orders," Miss Curtis smiled. "About Knight because you'll get too little, about his enemies because you'll get too much. Knight never talks much about himself. I can get his personal file, and that's about all you'll get. For the other, I think you'd better narrow it down, at least at first. This slot-machine case was his last big story. Why don't we assume for the time being that's where we ought to look? And if we don't come up with something, we can always go further back."

This sounded agreeable to Ronald, and he consented. As Miss Curtis was about to leave the office to get the files, he said, "Do you have a copy of that Short Vincent story Knight wrote? Burnett recommended that I read it."

"In the folder in the left-hand drawer," she replied, and left the room. Ronald found the clipping without much trouble and read:

Short Vincent Knows
By Barry Knight
There is a street in our town named Vincent Street, but more often called Short Vincent. Although located in the busy downtown section, it connects with two streets that are not main arteries, and so is comparatively little known.

Hemmed in by tall buildings, little sunshine penetrates here. It is a street of some top-grade hotels and some of lesser repute; of restaurants and bars; of back entrances to some famous enterprises and ménages.

Want to know Short Vincent? Put on your best suit, enter one of the restaurants there, have a good meal, and come out again—and you will have noticed nothing strange. But try it another way: Wear that older blue serge that's just a little shiny, your heels a little rundown, your hair a little straggly. Sit on a stool in the restaurant instead of at a table, and give Short Vincent a chance to look you over and feel you out. Then maybe it'll decide you belong.

Short Vincent is no Skid Row; it's proud of its dignity. There are no brawls and few drunks. Hardly any of its denizens have criminal records of consequence. Your wallet is as safe here as it would be on Park Avenue. Got a few loose bucks? Short Vincent will be glad to relieve you of them, and you'll have a good time the while. That's only sharp. But pickpocketing? Don't be silly. That would be dishonest!

What do you want at a bargain price? Short Vincent can get it for you wholesale, for everybody knows somebody who knows somebody who... Want to put down two bucks on the third race? Short Vincent wouldn't dream of taking it, but there's a fellow who knows a fellow... Point spots on the sports contests? Short Vincent knows them all, and one suspects that most of them were calculated right here.

Why didn't Avila try a squeeze bunt in the ninth inning against the Yankees? The sports writers don't know. The people who watched from the stands or on television don't know. But Short Vincent knows the reason. One reason? Nay, that would be doing Short Vincent an injustice. Short Vincent knows a dozen reasons, mutually contradictory and all equally implausible.

How's the jury going to decide? Acquittal, of course. Short Vincent knows. Something that got past the judge, the third juror is the strangled wife of the victim's second cousin. How does Short Vincent know? Nobody knows. Short Vincent will be glad to tell you anything at all—except how Short Vincent found out. That is each individual's secret, no matter what incredible explanation he may offer.

In short, Short Vincent is a street of guys who are in the know. It is a seething, whirling hotbed of rumor. Absurd, impossible? That has no meaning here. Even the fantastic becomes the rational when passed along in a whisper.

Friends do not always speak on Short Vincent. One friend will offer a tentative glance, which the other may accept or reject. And then they may decide to speak—but no names, please; it's better not to use names. And the first cool breeze sends coat collars up and hat brims slouching down. On Short Vincent everybody looks the part.

What are these characters after, anyway? Money? No one's getting rich on Short Vincent.

Prestige? There's little of that here; the stuffed shirt would be better advised to stay home. The kingpin of the moment is the guy with the hottest tip, the latest anecdote, the most incredible gossip. "Connections"—that is the thing that gives each man his moment in the sun, and so becomes the secret he would guard with his life.

And that, perhaps, is the best explanation of Short Vincent. Not understanding themselves, these guys cannot be understood by others; they lose themselves in extrospection to avoid the necessity of introspection; guys with a heart, with reasonable success, but still lacking something, and so they supplement their daily existence by the vicarious thrill of being in the know.

Queer, Ronald thought, hardly knowing whether he ought to smile or not. In the newspaper business you expected to run into some odd ducks, but he had never before encountered a whole collection of them quite like this. Before he could speculate further, Miss Curtis returned with an armful of folders.

The personal file was by far the smaller, and Ronald gave it his first attention. As Miss Curtis had told him, there wasn't much. It appeared that Knight had come to the city immediately after graduating from high school, and this was his first job. There was a warm, friendly letter of introduction from a minister, reading simply:

TO WHOMEVER IT MAY CONCERN:
I have known Barry for a number of years, and he enjoys my highest trust and confidence. I am certain that he will adequately fulfill any tasks for which he may covenant.
Faithfully, Gerald Milton, D.D.

The letter was typewritten on the letterhead of a church in the village of Imperial. The typing was a little uneven, with a number of erasures, suggesting that the minister himself might have typed it, rather than a trained secretary. However, as far as Ronald could tell, everything seemed to be in good order.

"Was this reference ever checked?" he inquired.

"I'm not sure, but probably not. An eighteen-year-old boy isn't likely to have much of a past to conceal—at least, not a neat-appearing, ambitious boy who proves himself completely competent for his job. I think you'll agree that Doctor Milton was right, that Knight has certainly been more than adequate."

Ronald laid the letter aside. Very likely there wasn't much use checking a reference like this. Almost everyone can find someone who will write a nice letter about him, and there were no past employers, who might have proved more critical. Since the letter could hardly be a forgery, Dr. Milton must have signed it in good faith. However, without implying any criticism of the ministry, Ronald's past experience was that ministers are more likely to forgive people than to judge them, a quality of faith that sometimes sets them apart from the general population.

And that was really about all the personal file had to tell him, the remainder of the papers being nothing more than a cut-and-dried summary of Knight's service on the newspaper. He turned his attention to the other file. Ronald was already familiar with the series of articles on the slot-machine racket, as they had appeared in the paper, but the file supplied a good many items of background that were missing from the published accounts. As usual, Knight had pulled no punches. He showed no hesitancy about mentioning names, and the name that popped up more often than any other was that of Freddie Uglancie. The implication was that Uglancie, now a respected citizen living in Shaker Heights, was actually the leader of slot-machine operations in the entire state.

Yet, oddly, when Ronald tried to check this charge, he could find virtually nothing in the file to sustain it.

"Miss Curtis, are these *all* the papers?" he questioned.

She looked at him oddly. "Of course not, Ronald. Knight had a collection of private papers that even I have never seen."

"Where are they, at his home?"

"Certainly not. They're in a special compartment in the office safe, to which only Knight has a key."

"Well, what are the nature of these papers? Have you any idea?"

"Oh, yes, I could make a good guess. In his newspaper stories Knight only wrote as much as he could prove. He must have had a good deal of other information that he couldn't prove—anyway not yet—and that information might prove very valuable to certain people."

"People like Freddie Uglancie?"

"That's about what I had in mind," she admitted.

Ronald thought the matter over carefully, before remarking slowly, "Then it looks like this Freddie Uglancie may be the best lead we have so far. So what do I do about it?"

"Why not call him up and ask him for an interview?"

Ronald thought she was joking, but saw in a moment she wasn't. "He'd never see me."

"How do you know? You don't take anything for granted in this business." She reached for the phone. "Want me to try?"

Ronald shrugged. "What's there to lose?"

Asking for an outside line, Miss Curtis dialed the number, then turned the phone over to Ronald. Someone, apparently a servant, answered the phone, and when Ronald asked for Mr. Uglancie, the connection was switched.

"Hello?"

"Mr. Uglancie? This is Ronald Wilford of the *Star.* I'd like to have an interview with you, if I may."

"Why, certainly, Mr. Wilford," Uglancie responded in a cordial voice. "Would eleven o'clock be convenient?"

"Perfectly. Thank you," and Ronald replaced the receiver, puzzled. He had his interview with Uglancie, and now wondered almost desperately what on earth he would be able to say to him.

CHAPTER 3

An Unsatisfactory Interview

Because the rapid transit would get him out to Shaker Heights faster, Ronald did not stop for his car, but went directly to the terminal. Within half an hour he stood before Uglancie's fine suburban home and rang the door chimes. He was admitted by a servant, and after a short wait Uglancie came into the room.

"Well, Wilford," he beamed, extending his hand, "I haven't had the pleasure of meeting you yet, but I'm sure we're going to get along fine."

"How do you do, Mr. Uglancie," Ronald responded, rising and accepting the hand. Although Uglancie wasn't the kind of man for whom he had a great deal of respect, having accepted the hospitality of Uglancie's home, it was necessary to observe the social proprieties.

"I hope you don't mind my calling you Wilford," Uglancie went on, "and I hope you'll call me Freddie. Everybody does. It sounds so much friendlier."

"Thank you, Mr. Uglancie," said Ronald pointedly. It would have been too easy to forget the sort of man Uglancie was, to accept the friendship he seemed to be offering and then regret it afterward.

"Let's sit down," Uglancie urged, apparently choosing to ignore Ronald's rebuff. "I know you newspaper boys are always in a rush, but it won't hurt you to relax once in a while. Can I get you anything to drink?"

"No, I don't care for anything, thank you." Ronald had seated himself opposite Uglancie, and there was a slight pause. This was the awkward moment, and Ronald didn't quite know how to begin. "I'm sure, Mr. Uglancie, that you've read the series of articles in the Star about you and the slot machines—"

"Don't say slot machines," said Uglancie with a pained look. "I know your headline writers have to compress words into a small space, but the correct term is coin-operated machines. Slot machines suggest gambling, the so-called one-armed bandits, and there are no such machines in this county, as far as I know."

"Possibly not in this county, at least not operating openly. But in some other counties it's fairly notorious—"

"But where they do exist," said Uglancie quickly, "it's because the people want them and the police tolerate them. Either the police, or a group of citizens acting through the police, could close them all down in half an hour. Anyway, I don't know what that has to do with me. I have no connections with these down-state operations, and I never did."

"Knight seemed to think otherwise."

"You know something?" said Uglancie, smiling. "I think Knight must have written those articles with a lawyer looking over his shoulder. He implied a great deal, but what he actually said was so carefully worded that my attorney didn't think it was any use plastering him with a libel suit. That's the vicious thing about newspapers. They can ruin reputations by hint and innuendo, without saying anything you can pin on them. Knight didn't say I was the slot-machine king. He only said I was the *alleged* slot-machine king, but he didn't say who alleged it, except himself."

"At least he was able to show your connection with the local coin-operated machines, as you call them."

"I've always been fascinated by those machines," said Uglancie seriously, "even as a kid. I used to stand by the hour and watch those little steam shovels operating. A lot of these machines render a very useful service. There are some that dispense a useful product, some dispense music, there are weighing machines, machines that represent a game of skill like the pinball machines, and some that are just interesting to watch in operation. You'd be surprised at all the different types of machines. You know how some people get frustrated when the machine outwits them? Well, there's one machine just coming out that provides a place below where the customer can kick it. Then a few seconds later, after the customer has turned away, the machine emits a raspberry call. The idea is to make the customer laugh."

Ronald wondered what his own reaction would be if he were a customer—probably come back and give the machine a harder kick, he thought.

"I hope we're going to become good friends," Uglancie went on. "Sometime when you've got a little time to spare, I'd like you to look over some of my catalogues. I think you'll agree that there's nothing vicious about machines like these."

"I don't think Knight objected to the machines themselves," Ronald remarked. "It was your manner of running your business he didn't like."

"And once again he was careful not to attribute any malfeasance to me directly," Uglancie pointed out. "I don't see how he could have, anyway. It's true I did own and service a couple hundred machines several years ago, but I've sold out. My only interest now is as a hobby."

"Apparently Knight didn't think so. It wasn't his habit to rake up old scandals. I'm sure he wouldn't have brought your name into it unless he felt you were still actively involved."

"Does that mean he's still after me?" The question was asked very smoothly, without a trace of rancor, so that Ronald was almost surprised into giving an answer. He caught himself quickly.

"I guess you'll have to ask Knight about that."

"There's nothing I'd rather do." Uglancie's manner remained politely calm, but his hard eyes were fastened squarely on Ronald. "Let's come off it, Wilford. I know exactly why you're here. Knight has run out on you, and you don't know why or where. So you've come here to try to pump me for information."

Ronald was startled. How could Uglancie know any such thing, unless...? "Does that mean you have anything to do with his leaving town?"

"I didn't say that," said Uglancie coolly. "In fact, I'll go so far as to say just the opposite. I don't know where he is now, or why he left. But I'd very much like to find out. I owe Knight a score or two. Whenever anybody hits me, I try to hit him back just a little harder if I can."

"Is that a threat?" Ronald demanded. "If it is, you can save your breath. You have a fine home, a family, servants, two fancy cars out in the garage. You've won a certain acceptance in the community. I'm sure you'd like to hang on to all that. The community tolerates you so far, but you know you have to play it pretty carefully so it will continue to do so. I don't think either Knight or I need to be afraid to go out on dark nights."

"You're right there," said Uglancie quietly. "I have managed to acquire a certain standing in the community that I intend to hang on to at all costs. It would be a good thing for you to bear that in mind." He added quickly, "Now don't go getting worked up again. That's no threat. If you knew me better you'd know I never make threats; what's the use? If I intend to do something I do it, and why tip off the other party in advance? However, neither you nor Knight has anything to worry about from me—anyway, not in the way you mean. I never resort to violence—"

"Not even in Blassingham County early last summer?" questioned Ronald.

"That was an entirely different matter," said Uglancie carelessly. "When I'm hit, I do hit back, and sometimes I'm not always particular if I hit a little low. But I do *hit back*. It might be just as well to remind your friend Knight of that, in case he ever considers using the rest of the material he's got stored away in the third locked drawer on the right-hand side of your office safe."

Once again Ronald was amazed. How could Uglancie know all this? Did he have a source of information within the newspaper office itself? Uglancie leaned back, took out his cigarette case, and after making a gesture toward Ronald, took one himself and lighted it. Only then did Ronald see that Uglancie's hand was trembling. Beneath his appearance of calm, he must have been a very worried man. Ronald looked around the room, at the expensive period furniture, thick carpeting, rich draperies, and a number of paintings on the wall that appeared to be originals, and he thought: What's the use of all this, if you're going to be nervous about it?

"You appear to be a fine young man, Wilford," Uglancie went on, his tone once more smooth and syrupy. "I could tell you a lot about yourself, perhaps more than you even know yourself. You're a small-town boy, come to make good in the big city. You've still got the stars in your eyes, still convinced this is a great, big, wonderful world, except for a few minor flaws that you expect to correct singlehandedly."

"I don't see anything wrong with a person's having ideals," Ronald broke in.

"Of course not. I like to see it, particularly in a young person. But while your eyes are blinded with stars, it's a good idea to remember that you've got two good feet that ought to remain firmly planted on the ground. That's the first rule of journalism, or if it isn't, it ought to be."

He continued, as Ronald made no comment, "You were born and raised in Forestdale and attended school there. You were a student leader, served on the newspaper, ranked high in your class. After graduating you served a hitch in the army, then went to work for the town newspaper. You have a younger brother named Ted, and with him you were engaged in two investigations that brought you some passing mention in the national press. That's very good going for a small town."

Further details about Ronald's past life flowed smoothly from his lips, as Ronald grew more and more astonished. A few of the details were inaccurate, but most of it was accurate enough. He could tell that Uglancie had gone to a great deal of trouble and expense to learn all he could about Ronald. But why, what purpose did it serve?

"And now shall I tell you a little about Miss Curtis?" Uglancie proceeded. "Did you know she has a twin sister with whom she doesn't get along well?"

A twin sister! Then the woman who had looked him over so coolly wasn't Knight's secretary at all. You often hear people say, it must have been my twin, but just once in a thousand times it may happen to be true.

All the same, Ronald didn't feel that he ought to be picking up details like this from Uglancie.

"I don't think I want to hear anything more about Miss Curtis," he objected. "All these things you've told me, I suppose, are the kind of things almost anyone could find out, if he wanted to go to the bother. But now that you know, what good does it do you?"

"In your case, none at all, for the time being—although I can't be sure but what you might get in my hair sometime in the future. Quite frankly, Wilford, I don't care two pins about you at this moment. All I care about is Knight, and anybody who may be associated with him. I want to know all there is to know about Knight, every detail about his past life, I want to know him so well that I'll know what he's think-ing at almost any given moment. Now here's my proposition, Wilford. You don't like me. I'm sorry about that, but it's only because you don't understand me. Twenty years from now you'll be able to understand me better. But liking me isn't important. We're in a position where we both want the same thing. You want to find Knight, and so do I, so why don't we join forces, pool our efforts, so to speak?"

"No, thank you, Mr. Uglancie," said Ronald, rising to his feet. "I wouldn't care to make a bargain I might want to back out of later. It was courteous of you to grant me an interview, but I don't think I'll be bothering you again."

On his ride back downtown, Ronald did some heavy thinking. If Uglancie was sincere (but could you count on it?), he had had nothing to do with Knight's disappearance. One of the two leads Ronald had depended on had snapped in his hand, but he still held the other. The logical thing to do, then, was to follow the other thread, that letter of rec-ommendation from Dr. Milton. But as he thought it over, Ronald felt less certain that this was another thread at all. Maybe the two were entwined together. Uglancie was interested in uncovering Knight's past, too, and apparently he hadn't gotten very far, for he had asked Ronald to help him. But Ronald hadn't gotten very far himself. The only clue he held was Dr. Milton's letter, but seemingly this was a clue Uglancie, for all his sources of information, was lacking. Ronald was beginning to feel this letter might prove to be very important.

He stopped for lunch in the terminal, then returned to the office. He reported his failure, if it was a failure, to Miss Curtis, and could tell she was very disappointed.

"Then I suppose, Ronald, that it's something tied up with one of his previous cases."

"It might be," Ronald agreed slowly, "and I suppose it would be a good idea for you to check back through the files to see what you can find. Somehow I don't think that's the answer. This all came about too suddenly. If it does have anything to do with Knight's investigations, it's more likely to be some new investigation that we don't know anything about. I'm going to follow a little different lead. I'm going to drive down to Imperial this afternoon. If I don't uncover anything, I'll be back tomorrow. If I do, it'll probably take me longer."

He hesitated, as he started to leave. "I didn't know that you had a twin sister, Carole."

She looked up at him in surprise. "And I didn't know that you even knew I had a first name."

"Oh, I've known that for a long time. Only when I met this girl coming down the steps a couple of times, and she didn't say hello, I thought that—"

He felt his cheeks growing red.

"It's an odd thing," she covered up smoothly, "Karen and I don't dress alike, so women never confuse us. It's only the men that do."

"I suppose I wouldn't have, except that she was coming out of the office, and then—"

"Karen often stops in during her lunch hour. I suppose you heard that we didn't get along? There's never been any serious difference between us, except that we each feel we'd like to preserve our individuality. Don't you ever quarrel with your younger brother?"

"Mm, not very often—not since he got big enough to hit back."

It was necessary for Ronald to procure his suitcase from the editor's office. Burnett was in and asked how he was coming, and Ronald supplied the details.

"Are you sure Uglancie wasn't just acting?" asked Burnett.

"If he was, he ought to get the Academy Award."

Ronald had forgotten that he had left his suitcase just around the end of the editor's desk. He stumbled across it, and the suitcase burst open with a bang. The editor looked at him grimly, but didn't say anything.

Gathering his effects together, Ronald hurried out. And so, without ever having returned to his apartment in Bratenahl at all, he found himself on the treacherous ice-marred paving of Route 42 as he headed once more out of town.

CHAPTER 4

The Man Who Never Existed

Mrs. Milton received him cordially and invited him in, but when he inquired for Dr. Milton, she responded:

"My dear, then I suppose you haven't heard. Doctor Milton passed away two years ago."

"I'm sorry," Ronald murmured.

"I'm sure you mean that, young man, but you needn't be. Doctor Milton lived a full and useful life, and I shall be joining him very soon." Faith and hope shone triumphantly in her eyes.

Ronald could think of nothing to say except to proceed to business. "Mrs. Milton, did you ever know a person—a boy or young man—named Barry Knight?"

"Barry Knight?" Her brow puckered as she tried to recollect. "No, the name doesn't sound at all familiar to me."

"Well, then, is it possible that your husband knew him?"

"Oh, yes, that's quite possible. Doctor Milton knew a good many people whom I didn't know."

"This Barry Knight is said to have graduated from the local high school about six years ago."

She brightened. "Oh, then, that makes it very possible. You see, this is a fairly small village, and I think I know everyone who lives here. And I also know everyone in our congregation, whether they happen to live in the village or not. But the high school is different. Students come in from a large area around here. If they lived outside of town, and their families were not members of our church, then I might not ever meet them. But my husband might, for he was often concerned with school affairs."

Ronald produced the letter of recommendation her husband had written and showed it to her. "The question on my mind, Mrs. Milton, is whether your husband really wrote this letter."

"Yes, I would think so," she returned, after studying it carefully for a few moments. "This is our regular church stationery, and that looks like my husband's signature. Yes, I think I can say almost positively that my husband wrote this letter."

"I notice that there are no stenographer's initials on it. Does that mean that he typed the letter himself? Please excuse me for questioning you on all these details, but I feel the matter is very important."

"I think he must have typed it himself. Notice how short it is. If it had been a long letter, or a matter of great importance, my husband would probably have dictated the letter to the church secretary over the telephone, but a letter like this he could handle by himself. I can almost imagine how it must have happened. You say this young man had just graduated from school. Wanting a recommendation, I suppose he came to my husband and asked for it, and Doctor Milton agreed. He took the young man into the study, got out his old portable, and typed up the letter. He could manage pretty well with his two fingers, even though you can see that he did make some mistakes."

Ronald hesitated. "Please excuse me once more, Mrs. Milton, for suggesting anything unpleasant, but may I assume that your husband really did have a long acquaintance with Barry Knight—that it wasn't just a casual friendship?"

"Doctor Milton says in his letter that he knew Barry for a number of years," said Mrs. Milton warmly, "and if he said it, you may be certain it was so. Doctor Milton tried to give people a helping hand when he could, but he always felt that nothing useful is ever accomplished with a lie."

"Yes, Mrs. Milton," Ronald agreed quickly, "I'm quite certain it must have been so." But he could not help but wonder why Barry had come to Dr. Milton for a recommendation, when he was not a member of the local church. Was it because there was no one else he could turn to? Had he been completely frank with the minister, or could he, perhaps, have managed to dupe him if he wanted to? But why should he want to do that? Just the fact that Mrs. Milton didn't remember Knight was nothing very substantial against him. But why, again, was so little known about Barry Knight's early background, why had Uglancie been unable to find out?

"Thank you, Mrs. Milton, you've been very helpful to me. As I mentioned before, it's very important that I should find Mr. Knight just as soon as I can, and I thought talking to some people who had known him in years past might be helpful to me."

"I'm only sorry I couldn't help you more. I won't ask you why you want to find Mr. Knight, for I'm certain it's none of my business, and it couldn't be anything disreputable if he was a friend of my husband's. I wish you good luck just the same. I suppose it must be very bad driving?"

"The snowplow has been through, and I have snow tires," Ronald reassured her. "I must be on my way. Good evening, and thank you once more."

Outside, he hesitated only a moment. His failure to secure anything very definite hadn't discouraged him, but instead had alerted him to a possibly bigger story. It was dark already, and to return to the city that night would have meant a long drive over bad roads. Besides, he was fully convinced that another day in Imperial might prove very profitable. If Mrs. Milton didn't know Knight, who did? The high school was probably the next place to check, but it was too late to do anything more that night. He got a room at the village's small hotel, and after catching up on some correspondence, turned in early.

Although this was still Christmas vacation, the school's secretary was at work when he arrived at the office to inquire. When he asked about Barry Knight, she consulted her files for a moment, then said:

"I'm sorry, but there was no one named Barry Knight in the graduating class you mentioned. Look here."

She produced a graduation day program, listing the names of all the persons graduating that year. Barry Knight's name was not given.

"It's just possible there's been a slight error. Is it possible that he may have graduated a year or two either before or after this date?"

But Ronald knew there had been no error, at least as far as he was concerned. Rather, he was testing another little theory of his. When a person tells a lie—if Knight had really gone to considerable trouble to conceal his past—then it was possible that he was telling at least *part* of the truth. This helps provide an authentic background, little details that can be swiftly filled in when the need arises.

The secretary consulted her files for another minute or two. "I'm sorry, but we've never had a student here named Barry Knight," she said, bursting his little theory beyond repair.

"Thank you," returned Ronald, a little disappointed, but more than ever convinced he was on the trail of a story bigger than had at first appeared. He held up the graduation program. "Do you mind if I take this with me?"

"Certainly not, by all means." She looked at him curiously. "So you're a reporter on the *Star*. You must find your work just fascinating."

Ronald was a little puzzled how to answer. To him newspaper work had lost most of its luster. It was a job, not too well paying, irregular hours, and a lot of running around, often with nothing to show for it but rebuffs, frustrations, and the ire of people who felt he was intruding upon them. But there was another side of it, too, though there were times when he was hard put to describe it. Just once in a while there was the satisfaction of a job well done, a story run down that seems to accomplish something useful. Maybe after all it was mostly the thrill of being "in the know," like the Short Vincent characters he had been hearing so much about.

"It has its moments," he admitted. "I guess the truth of it is, I'd never be caught doing anything else, if I could help it."

"Have you ever interviewed any of those big-time gangsters?" she asked breathlessly, as though reluctant to let him go.

"Not since yesterday," he answered glibly, and it startled him a moment later to reflect that what he had said was exactly the truth.

"I'd sometimes thought I'd like to try newspaper work myself," she offered, "but I suppose it must be terribly hard."

"No, not so hard," Ronald replied, "but it does take a certain type of personality. I don't know exactly how to describe it, but I guess you have to be the kind of person who believes that today is more important than tomorrow or yesterday. After all, today is all that we ever have."

She had been raised in a small town, like himself, and he felt a kindred sympathy for her. Besides, she didn't seem particularly busy, and it was comfortable inside and cold and blustery outside, and he hadn't quite decided what he wanted to do next. So he talked about newspaper work with her for another ten or fifteen minutes.

"If you're ever in the city," he invited, "why not stop in and I'll show you around the plant. And if nobody ever heard of Ronald Wilford, ask for Hayseed, and they'll know who you mean."

He could grin about it now, but in his first few weeks on the job that nickname had been hard to take. Still, if a little thing like that was going to break him down, it was best for the newspaper to know it right from the beginning. He seldom heard the nickname any more.

But after all, he and the secretary both had other work to do, and he finally left. He stood outside for a moment in the cold breeze buttoning up his coat.

Where to now? Mrs. Milton hadn't known Knight, he had never lived in the village as he had said, hadn't gone to school there. Yet Dr. Milton had known him well, even though it appeared no one else did. Could it be that that letter from the minister was a forgery? But Mrs. Milton had thought it was authentic, and surely she ought to know better than anyone else.

The village had a small library, and here Ronald was able to get copies of some old directories. No family named Knight had lived in the village or its surrounding territory in recent years. More and more Ronald was coming to the conclusion that Barry Knight was a man who didn't exist at all, that he had begun to exist only at that moment when he entered the newspaper office and asked for a job. Apparently there was no one, except a minister no longer living, who might have proved that Knight had existed before. So—what do you do when you're out hunting for a ghost?

When running into a dead end in a small village, Ronald often found it advisable to go to the local newspaper office, if there was one, and leaf through the files for the period he was interested in. It helped to give him the feel of the town, what people were thinking and doing and talking about. And he had no trouble finding out what people in Imperial were talking about at the time Knight was supposed to have graduated from high school. If the local newspaper was any reflection, all people were interested in was a robbery.

This was the robbery of a gasoline station near the edge of town. It was a small robbery by big-time standards, the sum involved being a little less than three hundred dollars. But the thing that made it outstanding was that the money was stolen by a man named Walter Desmond, a respected citizen of the community.

Walter Desmond was a man of middle years, an employee of Don's Service Station. It wouldn't be quite accurate to describe him as a ne'er-do-well, although it is true he never had much money. This came about partly through some personal misfortunes, and partly because he put so much time and effort into an invention he was working on, an invention he expected would make him rich and famous. Opinion was about equally divided in the village as to whether he was a genius or a crackpot.

On the night of the robbery, the proprietor had stopped off at the station at about ten o'clock, talked with Desmond briefly, and found everything in good order. Eleven o'clock was the usual closing time, and according to Desmond, he set the burglar alarm, locked up, and went home. Then, at about three o'clock the next morning the sound of shattering glass from a window in the station attracted attention. It was found that the window had been broken by a rock, but the prowler had apparently been scared off.

The proprietor was summoned. He unlocked the door and entered the station, which set off the burglar alarm, and by the time he could get it turned off half the people in the village were awake. With the burglar alarm still in good operating condition, it was quite a shock to him to open the cash register and find that about three hundred dollars was missing.

A little experimentation showed that no one could have entered the station through the broken window, even if there had been time. The hole wasn't large enough, and anyway the burglar alarm would surely have gone off. The alarm system was of the photoelectric-cell type. Simply breaking the window would probably not have set off the alarm. But any person trying to enter would have broken the invisible beam of light, which would have touched off the alarm. The police were able to show that no one could possibly have entered the building without setting off the alarm, unless he had first cut the wires of the alarm system. Apparently neither thing had happened. Even the proprietor himself could not enter the building, once the alarm was set, until the system automatically shut itself off at seven o'clock in the morning.

The police theory was that Desmond had taken the money from the cash register before closing up, then set the alarm and locked up and gone home. At three o'clock he had returned and broken the window. He intended to pick out the pieces to make a larger hole, then reach in until the alarm system went off, and quickly make his escape. It would then look like an outside robbery. Unfortunately for him, the breaking of the window had attracted attention, and he had been unable to complete his plan.

Although Desmond had not taken the stand in his own defense, the theory his lawyer tried to develop was that he had forgotten to set the alarm when he left. That later, burglars had entered, stolen the money from the register, and set the alarm system as they left. Why the window was broken was not explained, except as possibly the work of a mischievous boy.

The defense theory did not long hold up in court, when Don explained that setting the burglary system was no simple matter. Because the station was a little bit isolated, and there had been past robberies, Don had gone to the trouble of installing an expensive system. There were three boxes that had to be set each in proper turn, and this was done by the turning of a key. Only Don, and his employee, Desmond, had keys. The defense suggested the possibility that a duplicate key might have worked, but Don explained that even then the key had to be used correctly. Turning it the wrong way, or too far, would touch off the alarm. And the alarm box by the door had to be set last with the door open, for it was the closing of the door itself that threw it into operation. It seemed extremely unlikely that anyone could have set the system into operation unless he was familiar with it and had a proper key.

It was easy to see why the jury chose to believe the police theory rather than the defense's, and Walter Desmond was sentenced to a term of one to ten years in the state penitentiary.

It was an interesting case, Ronald thought, except that it didn't seem to have anything to do with finding Barry Knight.

"Well, what should I do, follow it up, or go home?" Ronald thought. He took a coin from his pocket. "Heads I go home, tails I stay." He flipped the coin, and it came down heads.

It was an inexcusable superstition for a newspaperman, except that he seldom did what the coin ordered. He turned the car about and headed toward the gasoline station.

CHAPTER 5

A Barrel of Walnut Shells

The sign over the gas station door still read "Don's Service Station." Probably the same proprietor, Ronald thought, for small enterprises tended to change names when they changed owners. The man who came out to render service had an air of proprietorship about him.

"You're Don?" Ronald questioned.

"That's right. How much will she hold?"

"Oh, I think five gallons will be enough."

Don busied himself at the tank for a couple of minutes, and by the time he was done, Ronald was out of the car and had come around to watch him.

"Say, that's a pretty low license number you got," Don remarked. "You somebody important?"

"No, I'm a newspaper reporter. The paper got the license for me."

As a matter of policy, Ronald never refused to give his name or state his profession to anyone who asked him. Partly it was because he felt he wasn't very successful in carrying out a bluff. At first he had thought that this inability to pretend to be something he wasn't might prove a handicap in the newspaper business, but as it turned out the results were just the opposite. People came to respect him for his sincerity, and tried to help him when they felt they could.

Don narrowed his eyes. "You down here on business?"

"Oh, there was a little something I've been checking into." Ronald nodded toward the station. "Is this where the robbery took place—that one six years ago?"

"Yep, this is the place. You dragging all that up again?"

"No, not exactly. I just stumbled across it while I was checking into something else."

"Well, if you want to write it all up again, I don't care. There were plenty of stories about it at the time, but I guess it's all old stuff by now. I can't show you how my alarm system works, because I had to change it around after I got all that publicity, but it's still on the same principle.

I installed it myself, kind of a hobby with me. Photoelectric eyes, three of them, set with a special key that you have to use in just the right way. And you have to set the eyes in the right order, too, because they're cross-beamed. If you set number two first, for example, you'd break the beam when you tried to set number one, and the alarm would go off. Another little gimmick, these eyes have batteries in them that are automatically switched on if the outside current is cut off. I got a different system for my pumps. I won't tell you what it is, but if anybody tried to steal some gas some night he'd be due for a big surprise. That's the idea of all these different kinds of systems—try to stay one jump ahead of the burglars."

"With these beams that you've got set inside, isn't it possible that if a person knew exactly how they were set, he might be able to jump over them or crawl under them?"

"Not at the angles I've got 'em set, not in my small station. A burglar'd have to be the world's champion jumper, or the world's champion creeper to get past 'em. No, the police looked it over, and they agreed it was burglarproof, unless the burglar somehow broke down the alarm system first. That didn't happen at the time of the robbery. Say, just what angle are you following up on this robbery, anyway?"

"I didn't exactly have an angle," said Ronald slowly. "I suppose the thing I wanted to know was whether there was any way that Walter Desmond might be innocent."

"Sure, there is," said Don promptly.

"There is?" Ronald exclaimed.

"Sure, I might have stolen the money myself."

"You?"

"That's right. Suppose Wally forgot to lock up the station that night. I come back and find it open. I go in and steal the money, and set the alarm on my way out. Later this kid breaks the window, which attracts attention, and the police come. I got a perfect case. Only thing you got left to explain is how come Wally forgot to lock up, and why would I want to rob my own cash register, and then send the money back to myself a couple of weeks later?"

"You got your money back?" asked Ronald in surprise.

"Yep, came mailed to me in a plain envelope. That was Wally's doing, of course."

"Wasn't he in jail by that time?"

"Oh, sure, but he must have had some friend on the outside who'd take care of it for him. Who else would send me three hundred dollars except Wally? A real screwball."

As Ronald turned this new fact over in his mind, Don studied him for a few moments, then laughed. "You don't really think I'd rob my own station, do you?"

"You weren't insured against robbery?"

"Nope. These burglar alarms are all the insurance I need." He nodded proudly toward the station house.

"Then it doesn't sound very likely, unless you had some grudge against Desmond."

"Him? You're barking up the wrong tree there, mister. That's not my way of doing business. If I had it in for somebody, I might give him a poke in the jaw, but I wouldn't send him to jail. I like to handle those things for myself. Anyway there couldn't be anything like that with Wally. He was as harmless as they come—or anyway, that's what I thought up until the robbery. Big, open face, older man needing a job—I didn't even bother checking his references when he came. Ordinarily a fellow like me has two or three kids hanging around. They work cheap, but it's not all profit. When you can get a responsible older man at a reasonable wage, you're so much ahead. That's the way it looked to me. And then at the trial it all came out that he had a criminal record before. I never would have thought it. It just goes to show that you can't trust anybody—but anybody."

"Was Desmond earning good wages here?"

"Good enough. He put in long hours, picked up quite a bit of overtime. He could have got by easy, except that he was putting so much money into his invention. Always puttering around with it as soon as he had a spare minute. I never had any reason to complain, though."

"What kind of invention was it," Ronald questioned, "or did he keep that part of it a secret?"

"Oh, I don't think it was much of a secret. It was a new kind of storage battery that was supposed to last for the life of your car. I don't think he ever got it operating very well. He talked it over with me a little, but I didn't understand very much about it."

He shrugged. "Maybe he really had something, I don't know. I suppose they laughed at Thomas Edison, too. A screwball, but what's the difference? I'm a screwball, you're a screwball. Know what I got home in my attic? A barrel full of walnut shells. Not good for one blamed thing in all creation as far as I know, but I got 'em. Collected 'em when I was a boy, I don't know why, but every time I start to throw them out I remember how much work I went to collecting 'em."

"Do you happen to know whether Desmond is still in prison?"

"Nope, haven't seen him since the trial. What did he get, one to ten years, wasn't it? Chances are he's been out for years. They wouldn't hang on to a guy like that any longer than they had to. Never came back around here, though. Sort of wish he would, 'specially if he needs a job."

"You'd hire him again?" asked Ronald incredulously.

"Sure, why not? I don't care, as long as I got my money back."

"If you've got so much confidence in him, why do you suppose he robbed you in the first place? Was he badly in need of money?"

"No, I don't think so." Don leaned forward confidentially. Ronald was used to this attitude by now. People whispered things in a reporter's ear, then expected to see it next day on the front page. "I think he wanted to go to jail. Look how he stole the money so that everybody'd know he did it, and how he hardly put up any defense, and how he returned the money afterward. He must have *wanted* to go to jail, so he could work on his invention in peace and security."

Ronald's hand went into his pocket. He took out a dime and handed it to Don. "Thanks, Don, I appreciate your help. That's not a tip. Try it out for luck. I've just resigned from the screwballs."

He drove off, as Don stared first at the coin in his hand, and then at the fast-receding car.

Ronald's next objective was already clear in his mind. It seemed to be an open-and-shut case against Walter Desmond, and there was no reason for him to follow it up further, except that he was becoming more than ever convinced that Barry Knight had been interested in the case.

Imperial was not far from the state capital, and Ronald decided he might just as well drive on and see what he could find out about Desmond at the prison. He entered the bleak walls in the middle of the afternoon and had no trouble securing an interview with the assistant warden, just inside the first of the three locked gates.

"Walter Desmond?" said the assistant warden thoughtfully. "Yes, I remember him very well. He was paroled just a few months ago."

"What sort of man was he?" questioned Ronald.

"Oh, Desmond was a model prisoner, never gave us any trouble at all. Always busy, always cheerful. He was the sort of man who makes my job a little easier. It will be a great surprise to me—and I might say a great shock—if he ever comes back to prison again. I recommended him for parole a number of times."

Ronald felt puzzled. "You say you recommended him for parole before this, and yet his parole only recently came through?"

"Yes. I say I recommended him, but Desmond himself refused to apply for parole. He felt that he wasn't quite ready to face the outside world. We don't try to rush that sort of thing—we feel a man like that is in a better position to judge himself than we are."

"Isn't that rather an unusual reaction?"

"Unusual, yes, but not unheard of. You'd be surprised how many men are in here because prison gives them a sense of security they'd never been able to find in the outside world."

Six years, Ronald was thinking, six years. What did six years do for a man that five or four wouldn't do? Was that the time Desmond needed to bring his invention to perfection?

"You mentioned that Desmond was very busy. Would it be asking too much to inquire just what it was that was occupying his time?"

"No, I don't think so. It was an invention of his, something to do with storage batteries. I'm not personally acquainted with the details, but he had the help of some men who are more mechanically inclined than I am. Their opinion was that he had hold of an important new principle. Naturally I gave him all the encouragement I could—something like that goes far to hasten a man's rehabilitation."

"Then would you say this was a pretty valuable invention?"

"I'd hardly go that far," said the older man cautiously. "It had possibilities, but it needed further perfection. Desmond couldn't seem to arrive at quite the best combination of metals, and our facilities here for metallurgy are extremely limited. He had gone far enough so that he could procure a patent, but the battery would be of no commercial importance until it was improved. That would probably require a large sum of money, and the sponsorship of someone who had a great deal of confidence both in Mr. Desmond and in his invention. I hope that Desmond will somehow find the right man."

"Then you know where Desmond is right now?"

"Oh, yes, our parole records would show that. However, our rules do not allow me to make such information public. But if you had a message you wanted to get to Desmond, perhaps I could see that it reached him."

"No," said Ronald slowly, "I don't think I have any message for him that he would be likely to answer. He wouldn't know me at all, and would probably think I was just trying to give his case more publicity." He deliberated the matter in his mind. "Did Desmond ever claim he was innocent, or anything like that?"

"Why, no. I don't think anything like that ever came up. Most of our men claim to be innocent, but they seldom expect anyone to believe them. I never heard Desmond make any such claim at all, not even in his application for parole. Fortunately, I might add, for a thing like that counts against a man, makes it look as though he hasn't learned his lesson."

"And yet I suppose that you do occasionally have an innocent man in here?" Ronald inquired. "I don't want to be argumentative. It was just a philosophical point."

"And I'll try to answer in the same spirit, Wilford. Can an innocent man go to prison? It would be very difficult, for under our system of law an accused man is presumably given the benefit of every doubt. By innocent men I do not wish to include those who might possibly be mentally incompetent, or have a long record of social irresponsibility, or whose motives for doing what they did are open to interpretation.

"I would regard a man as innocent only if he actually did not commit this particular crime or any other major crime, does not know who did it, and is at a loss to explain the chain of circumstances that seem to prove his guilt. This might come about through a mistaken identification, or a remarkable series of coincidences, or the deliberate attempt of another person to plant evidence against him. Apparently none of these particular circumstances apply to Desmond, and so I must regard him as guilty. It may be that there are one or two or three truly innocent persons within this prison, but I sincerely hope there are not."

The man to whom Ronald was talking was a man of vast experience in the field of criminology, and Ronald respected his opinion. That seemed to be final. Walter Desmond was guilty. The evidence was solid, everyone was convinced of his guilt, even Desmond himself did not protest very loudly. When he had a chance to get out of jail, he had asked instead to be allowed to stay in! But if Desmond was guilty, what was Ronald doing down here, anyway?

"There's just one more thing on my mind. Did Desmond have any visitors, any correspondence, anyone who seemed to be interested in him?"

"Apparently there was only one person, a man by the name of Dixon Orlando. He stopped in every two or three months, appeared to be Desmond's only contact. I was very much disappointed that Desmond would have an acquaintance like that. I went to some trouble to look Orlando up. It seems that he has no criminal record, but he knows his way around the underworld altogether too well to suit me. I sincerely hope that Desmond hasn't tied up with him again."

He shook his head slowly. "That was just one of the many things I never understood about Desmond, but the thing that bothered me the most was this: what was a man like Desmond doing in prison, anyhow?"

As Ronald drove north toward home he could not avoid a feeling of elation. After all his trouble, after all his apparently fruitless inquiries, he had finally struck pay dirt at the last moment. He had definitely proved a link between Barry Knight and Walter Desmond, and that link was Dixie Orlando.

CHAPTER 6

An Unexpected Visitor

"Good news, Carole," Ronald announced to his fellow worker. "I finally came up with something."

"But you didn't find Barry Knight?"

"Oh, no, there's no such person as Barry Knight. Doctor Milton is dead, and Mrs. Milton doesn't remember him. Here—here's a list of all the persons in his supposed high-school class, and his name isn't on it. I'm convinced that Barry Knight doesn't exist. Do I sound crazy?"

"You sound very excited," she smiled. "Now what's this piece of good news you've come up with?"

As rapidly as he could, he explained about the gas-station robbery in Imperial, how Walter Desmond had been in the penitentiary, and that Dixie Orlando was his principal visitor.

"If I could only find that Orlando character," said Ronald, pacing restlessly around. "Don't you think, Carole, that maybe Burnett is wrong? If I only went down to Short Vincent—"

She disagreed with a quick shake of her head. "You wouldn't find him, Ronald, not if he didn't want you to find him. And it's more important than you know that a young reporter shouldn't make a mistake on Short Vincent. It might influence your whole career. Wait a while longer."

"What is this Short Vincent anyway? It's only a couple of blocks from here, and yet I've never been there. I'm beginning to believe it's a kind of never-never land that doesn't really exist. Someday I'm going to have to go down and see for myself. What do you say, Carole, how about having lunch with me someday on Short Vincent—after I get my first by-line?"

"I'd love to, Ronald. It's a date," Carole replied with a smile.

He inquired how she had been making out on the case, but she had nothing encouraging to report.

"I'm beginning to think it's hopeless, Ronald. There are so many things we can't know about. There have been a number of people who have been hurt by Knight's stories, but what about friends, relatives, people who have been hurt only indirectly? What about people who only imagine they've been hurt? We can never cover them all. I've picked out some of the most obvious names, but somehow it doesn't seem to me these are the kind of people Knight would be running away from."

"We don't know that Knight was running *from* something," Ronald pointed out. "He might have been running *to* something."

"Then why hasn't he come running back?"

"I've been thinking about that," said Ronald seriously. "How do we know that Knight ever intended to come back? Oh, I know, he left a few clothes and a violin in his room, but that doesn't seem important enough to make sure he'd return. Whatever was important enough to take him away might be important enough to *keep* him away."

She turned her chair toward him, but as he seemed too restless to sit down, she cleared a little space on the desk, so that he could strike the pose most characteristic of him.

"Ronald, what's your theory of all of this? I know you're not supposed to have a theory before you have some facts, but the facts we've gotten so far don't seem to be getting us anywhere."

"If I tell you you'll think I'm crazy. Call it a hunch if you want to, but I've got a strong feeling that for some reason Knight believes Desmond was innocent!"

She raised her eyebrows. "But how could he be? You said the evidence against him was conclusive."

"I know, I know. I've heard a dozen or more things that *prove* Desmond was guilty, and I haven't heard one single shred of evidence that would show he wasn't. Just the same Knight must have thought so. In some ways Knight reminds me of my brother Ted. Ted always believes everybody's innocent. If he stays in newspaper work, he's going to find out this is a cold world."

"But there are plenty of warm people in it, Ronald," she reminded him.

They returned to the consideration of the case. "How would Knight know all this, anyway, Ronald? You haven't been able to prove that Knight was connected in Imperial at all."

"No, not Knight, but someone—maybe Knight under a different name—who knew what was going on. I've read over that letter from the minister again, and I notice it only used Knight's first name. Maybe he had a different surname then."

"Is there anyone in his graduating class named Barry?"

He looked over her shoulder, but her finger ran down the list more rapidly than his eye could follow. No such name appeared.

"Then maybe both his names were different," Ronald suggested. "Maybe he went to the minister, and told how he wanted to change his name, and the minister agreed and wrote the letter."

"Would a minister do something like that?"

"You've got me there. Maybe he would, if he felt the circumstances justified it."

"But, Ronald, how was Knight concerned in the robbery? Maybe he did live in Imperial, maybe under a different name, maybe he did have his own ideas about what was going on. But why did it concern him?"

"Can you stand another wild flight into fancy?"

"I'd love to come along for the ride."

"Six years ago Knight was a boy of about seventeen. I've been trying to think how a boy would fit into this case, and maybe I've come up with something. As I see it there's only one way a boy would fit in. A number of people think that the window in the gas station was broken as a boy's prank, and I've got a hunch Barry Knight was the boy."

"But if it was a boy, he didn't have anything to do with the burglary, did he?"

"No, everybody agreed no one could have entered the station through the broken window. About the only difference it made was that the robbery was discovered in the middle of the night instead of the next morning."

"Who would have discovered it?"

"The owner, this man named Don, I suppose, when he came to work."

"Wouldn't the alarm ring when he went in? I know it wouldn't, but I mean there must have been some means of shutting it off."

"No, it was on clockwork, and shut itself off automatically at seven o'clock. I don't know what time the station opened, but I noticed a sign that it now opens at nine o'clock, so maybe it was the same then. At least there must have been some time gap, for the proprietor wouldn't want to take the risk of touching off his own alarm.

"Now think about that. A two-hour lapse between the time the alarm shut off and the proprietor came to work. Ordinarily he would have entered the station, and probably would never have noticed anything was wrong until he went over to the cash register and counted the money. Even then it would have been difficult for him to prove that Walter Desmond stole the money. Maybe a burglar broke in sometime after the alarm was switched off—this was autumn, and it would still be dark at seven o'clock. Maybe it would appear that Don himself stole the money. To my mind this makes the case against Desmond even more damaging. The question in everyone's mind was why he should steal the money in such a way that all the evidence pointed toward him, but this would help explain how he might have expected to get away with it.

"Now look how the broken window changed all that. The breaking of glass was heard, and the burglary was discovered during the night. This was the crushing blow in the evidence against Desmond. So it couldn't have been anyone except Desmond who stole the money. Even Don couldn't have stolen it, unless Desmond absent-mindedly forgot to set the alarm when he left, and Desmond made no such claim. More than anything else it was the broken window that sent Desmond to prison.

"Now let's try to see how all this would appear to Knight. He had broken the window as a foolish boyish prank, and now he suddenly finds that he has been the means of sending a man to prison. Wouldn't that fact weigh on his conscience? Seventeen is a particularly sensitive age. I know, because I can see it in Ted. Don't you think what happened would have a serious effect on Knight?"

"But what difference would it make, Ronald, as long as Desmond was really guilty?"

"That's just it, what difference would it make? And the only answer I can come up with is that Knight must have thought Desmond was innocent. Now I don't mean that Desmond was really innocent, only that Knight in his wretched state of mind was led to believe so. That would account for his later interest in the case—not so much to clear Desmond as to satisfy his own conscience."

"Well, you may be right, Ronald," she smilingly agreed, "but somehow it seems to me that we're only answering riddles with more riddles. I know Knight, and he is pretty levelheaded. This story of yours only becomes reasonable if Desmond was innocent, and that seems impossible."

After all his brilliant deduction, Carole's summary came as a letdown, and yet Ronald was forced to admit it was probably true. Perhaps, as so often happens, he had arrived at part of the truth, but only a part, and he couldn't tell which part was true. Maybe it was merely pride in his own creation, but he decided to hang on to his theory for a while until he saw what came of it.

Before he left the office, the telephone rang, and after answering it, Carole handed it to him.

"Ronald Wilford speaking."

"This is Mr. Carey." Carey was the manager at Ronald's apartment house.

"Yes, Mr. Carey."

"I didn't know whether you were back or not, Wilford. The heat is still shut down in your rooms."

"I came back to the city two days ago, but I haven't had a chance to get home yet. I'll be in tonight. Thanks for your interest."

"That's not what I called about. It's something else. There's a man here to see you. He wanted to get in touch with you, but of course I wouldn't tell him where you are working, or anything, without your permission."

"What does he want? Did he give a name?"

"No, that's just it, he won't give a name. Just says he has to see you, it's very important."

"What does he look like?"

"Elderly man, slender, not too tall, gray hair and not very much of it, carrying a suitcase."

"It doesn't sound like anyone I know. You're sure he's not a salesman?"

"Doesn't look to me like he's got any business at all. I'd guess he could use a good meal, and that suitcase looks like it contains all his worldly possessions. Oh, another thing, it's got the initials J.K. on it."

"J.K.! Listen, I think I'd better see him. Get him something to eat if he wants it, and get my rooms warmed up and let him sit in there, but sort of keep an eye on him. I'll be home just as soon as I can get there."

"A new lead?" asked Carole as he hung up.

"I don't know, it's just that I'm being very alert for anyone whose last name begins with K. If it turns out to be phony, I'll be back, but if it amounts to something, I'll do whatever seems best to follow it up."

He made the drive to his apartment in what must have been record time for such unfavorable driving conditions. He shared the apartment with another young man, a college student who was still away for the holidays. Pausing only long enough at the manager's office to express a word of thanks, he hurried on upstairs to his rooms. The door was open, and a man was sitting on the sofa.

Upon catching sight of Ronald, the man rose and came forward. He was dressed rather shabbily, and his face had at least a two days' growth of beard. When he walked, it was almost with a shuffle, and his manner was diffident. But Ronald had met enough people to know that many persons who adopt a pose of shyness and reserve are actually very forward and pushing about getting what they want. In their own quiet way, they are like the polite camel who drove his master out of the tent.

"Mr. Wilford?" the man asked hesitantly.

"That's right."

"I sure hated to bother you, Mr. Wilford, but—well, I guess there just wasn't anything else I could do. My son spoke about you many times. My name is Joseph Knight. I'm Barry Knight's father."

Ronald could hardly conceal his astonishment, although that letter K had helped prepare him for the surprise. But Barry Knight didn't have a family, everyone had said that about him. And this man looked very much neglected. Everything about him cried out to deny the relationship. Would Barry Knight have neglected his own father? Surely not knowingly, but maybe it wasn't knowingly. Maybe there was a lot more to the story than that.

"Is that so? Won't you sit down, Mr. Knight?"

"Thank you." The elderly man returned to the sofa and crossed his legs, then proceeded to drum his finger tips on his knee, apparently a habitual mannerism with him.

"Did Barry ever mention me to you, Mr. Wilford?"

"No, I can't recall that he did."

"No, no, I suppose he didn't," Mr. Knight returned with a sigh, almost as though talking to himself. "Well, the young are thoughtless, but I won't say anything more about it. There was blame on both sides."

His manner became more forward, and he leaned toward Ronald, pointing a finger and tapping it on his knee to emphasize his words. "But he did mention you, Mr. Wilford. Are you on the newspaper?"

"That's correct."

"Dear me, I didn't know that, though I began to suspect it from the way the manager acted when he called you. The way Barry spoke of you, I thought you were a friend rather than a business associate. That's why I came to you. I didn't want to go to the paper. I didn't think Barry would like me to go down there."

"I consider myself a friend of Barry Knight's just as much as a business associate," Ronald assured him, "and I'd do anything I could for you. If you'll tell me where Barry is, I'll be glad to put you in touch with him and help you to straighten out your difficulties, whatever they may be."

"Don't you know where he is?" The man's face showed his surprise. "That was the very thing I came here to find out."

CHAPTER 7

News from Short Vincent

Mr. Knight produced a wrinkled old sheet of paper with Barry's Franklin Boulevard address on it.

"I stopped out there to see what had happened to my son," he said, his voice trembling, "and they told me he wasn't there. Then I didn't know what to do. I didn't feel I ought to go to the paper. I wouldn't say that Barry is exactly ashamed of me, but—well, he has his own life to live, too. I tried to think who his friends might be, but he hardly ever mentioned anyone in his letters to me, and your name was the only one I remembered. And I remembered he had said something about an apartment in Bratenahl, but I didn't have the street address, and your name isn't listed in the telephone directory—you must be new here. But I came out here anyway, and tried a few buildings, until I was lucky enough to find the one where your name was listed. And so here I am."

"You're from out of town?" Ronald questioned.

"Yes, I live all by myself, a retired railroad man. That's why it doesn't cost me anything to travel. I got a lifetime pass. Barry used to write me regular every two weeks, and then when his letters stopped coming I figured I'd better mosey up here and see what the trouble was—I guess you know how it is."

Ronald could guess very easily. Every two weeks was payday, and Barry must have been sending a check to his father regularly. When the checks stopped coming, his father wanted to know why. There had to be some reason why Barry had never mentioned his father, and the reason was becoming embarrassingly clear. Could the fact that he wanted to avoid his father be the reason for Barry's leaving town? It didn't sound likely.

Nevertheless, Mr. Knight's greed offered Ronald an unexpected opportunity to check into some of the details of Barry's earlier life.

"The truth is, Mr. Knight, that I don't know where Barry is myself, and I'd like very much to find him. I don't want to pry into his personal affairs, but there might be something in his background that would give me a clue about why he left and where he has gone. Where did you and Barry live when he was small?"

"Barry and I live? I'm afraid you still don't understand the situation, Wilford. Barry's mother and I were separated when he was just a little shaver. I haven't seen Barry since he was hardly more than a towheaded toddler. Cute as tricks, it came near to breaking my heart when she took him away from me, but that's life. I won't say she didn't have some cause, but I won't say it was all my fault, either. There was blame on both sides. And then, I knew she'd bring up the boy to hate me, and so it just didn't seem right for me to keep coming to see him and opening up old wounds."

"Where did your wife and Barry live?" asked Ronald smoothly. If this man was a fraud, it would be a good idea to find out right at the start.

"They lived on a little farm down near Imperial. I wouldn't exactly call it a farm, but they had a few acres, enough for truck farming and such. They lived in with an older couple that didn't have any children of their own. Then when my wife died—let me see, Barry must have been about twelve or thirteen at the time—the couple kept Barry on and raised him till he got out of school."

"Didn't you try to see Barry, even after your wife died?" Ronald persisted.

"Well, no," said Mr. Knight lamely, "I made some inquiries, and he was getting along fine, and I figured out he was better off with them than he would be with me, especially since I traveled so much on the railroad. I sent him money whenever I could," he added quickly, "only times were bad, strikes on the railroad, and stuff like that."

Ronald nodded absently. He hadn't known of any railroad strike lasting five or six years, from the time Mrs. Knight died until Barry was out of school, and he wondered if Mr. Knight had ever sent home a single dollar toward his son's support.

"How did you finally get in touch with Barry again?" he asked.

"He was the one who got in touch with me. As I said, his mother brought him up to hate me, but as he got to be a man, I guess he came to wondering what his old man was like, and so he tracked me down. I let him know I was pretty hard up—bad leg wound got me retired from the railroad before I was of pension age—and he began to send me checks. A real right guy, in spite of what my wife told him. I always wanted to meet him, but somehow we never quite got together."

"Are you sure about all your information, about the little farm near Imperial?" asked Ronald, watching him closely.

"Oh, yes, I'm sure about that part of it," Mr. Knight answered confidently, "but for the rest of it I have to rely on what my wife said in her letters to me—and she never said much."

"Mr. Knight, I have reason to believe that Barry never lived in or near Imperial. What would you have to say to that?"

"Oh, he did, he did, I'm sure of that." He looked perplexed, then his brow cleared. "Oh, I know what you mean. It must be about the name. My wife and I were never divorced, but I know she went back to using her maiden name after she left me."

"What about Barry? What name did he go under?"

"Well, now, I never thought about that, but it would have been just like her to raise him under that name, too. Yes, sir, that would have been just like Ethel."

Then that was the explanation of it all, Ronald thought disappointedly. Barry Knight hadn't adopted a false name after leaving school. Instead he had gone back to using his own real name. He had confided his intention to Dr. Milton, and that accounted for the letter the minister had written. After all the romantic nonsense Ronald had been building up in his own mind about Barry's mysterious past, it seemed to be something very commonplace, sordid, and dull. Ronald almost wished he hadn't found out.

Mr. Knight's story answered another difficulty, too, for it placed Barry squarely on the scene at the time of the gas-station robbery. Ronald felt that his hunch on that part of it had been right, that Barry had broken the window maliciously, and therefore felt responsible for what had later happened to Desmond. He had continued to follow up the case through Dixie Orlando. Then where was Barry Knight now? He had gone to find Walter Desmond, clearly, either with the idea of clearing up an old injustice, or possibly for some reason having to do with Desmond's invention. The mystery was very nearly solved, except for a few details, such as why Knight had left without telling anyone, and whether he really had any intention of coming back.

"What was your wife's maiden name, Mr. Knight?" Ronald inquired.

The man's eyes flickered. "Johnson, Ethel Johnson. Yes, sir, that was the name she carried when I married her, and it was the name she went back to as soon as she got rid of me."

Johnson? Ronald didn't remember whether there was any boy named Johnson on that graduation program, but at least he knew there was no one named Barry. He remembered Carole's remark: "You answer a riddle with another riddle." It might have been interesting to go back to Imperial and check into the Johnsons, but he didn't feel he had time for that right now. His job was to find Barry Knight, and on that particular matter he still didn't know where to turn.

"Thank you, Mr. Knight. You've been very helpful. Where shall I get in touch with you in case I have anything to report?"

Mr. Knight looked very crestfallen. "I don't like to admit it, Mr. Wilford, but I don't have a dollar in my pockets—and I won't have until my next pension check comes through."

Well, what could Ronald do? He couldn't turn Mr. Knight out on the streets. No more could he put him on his newspaper expense account without permission. The easiest solution would be to give him a few dollars and tell him to go to a hotel, but he didn't quite like that answer either. Mr. Knight didn't seem like the kind of person who would do much to help himself if he felt there was someone else to help him. Besides, it wasn't possible for Ronald to dismiss a problem so easily, especially when it involved the destitute father of a good friend—and he had to admit that Mr. Knight had been helpful to him.

"You're welcome to stay here for a few days if you like, Mr. Knight. There's an extra bedroom until my roommate gets back. But it's only for a few days," he reminded him.

"Oh, certainly, Mr. Wilford, it won't be for more than a few days, I wouldn't dream of it. If I don't hear anything from my son by that time, I'll just have to think of something else. Where's the best place to apply for assistance in this town? The Travelers' Aid? Or would the County Welfare be better? Maybe the Red Cross would help me."

These characters always know their way around, Ronald thought in disgust. Well, if Mr. Knight imagined he could extend his visit beyond a few days, he would find himself badly mistaken, Ronald decided. Help these persons a little bit, and they get the idea they can count on you for everything. It was hard for Ronald to remember that this was the father of Barry Knight, a man who had befriended him on many occasions.

It seemed too late to bother about returning to the office that day. Anyway, he wasn't sure Mr. Knight had eaten for some time, and he himself was growing hungry.

"What do you think we'd better do for grub, Mr. Knight? I do some light cooking here, but when I want a good meal I usually go to a restaurant. Besides, I've been away, and I don't have very much in stock."

Mr. Knight opened the refrigerator door. "You've got bacon and eggs, and I see coffee and canned milk up on the shelf. That'll be plenty good enough for me—I'm not at all particular. But we ought to have bread."

"I'll run down to the delicatessen and pick up a few things," Ronald offered, glad to get away. He wanted to call Carole at the office, but didn't like to phone from home with Mr. Knight there. He looked around, remembering that Mr. Knight was a stranger to him. There wasn't anything of great value in the apartment, but walking over to his desk, Ronald found a few papers he didn't want Mr. Knight snooping into, and put them in his pocket. Then he went out, but thought it just as well to drop a word or two to Mr. Carey on his way past.

Carole was still at the office and was eager to hear about his visitor.

"Hold on to your hat, Carole," he advised her, "for it's none other than Barry Knight's father!"

"Ronald, are you sure?" she asked apprehensively. "Knight never mentioned his father to me."

"Well, I wouldn't care to vouch for this man's character, but a few details he gave me jibe with what we know already. As far as I know, no one but ourselves was on to that Imperial angle."

"Well, then, I guess you've got the case almost solved, if Mr. Knight can tell you everything you want to know about Barry."

"I didn't say that, Carole. It seems that he and his wife were separated when Barry was just a towheaded toddler, as he puts it. I don't think he'd even know Barry if he saw him,"

"Isn't it kind of late for him to be looking up his son after all these years?"

"Not for him. He's after money, of course. It seems that Barry has been sending him checks every payday, and now that the checks have stopped, he wants to find out why. I've got some more things to tell you, but I'll save them till morning. Meanwhile, there's one thing I'd like to know. See if you can find the name Johnson on that graduation list, will you?"

He waited half a minute, before she answered, "No, it isn't here."

He sighed, and she asked, "Does it matter very much?"

"No, I suppose not, but things would have been much simpler for us if it had been there. I seem to be always groping for something that jumps back out of reach just when I'm about to grasp it. How are you coming with your list of Barry's enemies?"

It was her turn to sigh. "It's growing by the minute. It would be a lot easier to make a list up of his friends."

Whatever Mr. Knight's failings in personality, they did not extend to his cooking, and Ronald found a delicious meal awaiting him, with bacon, eggs, and coffee done just right.

During the evening the telephone rang and Ronald answered.

"Hello?"

"Wilford?"

"Speaking."

"Say, Wilford, there's something I hear about you, but I don't know whether it's true or not. Is it the right dope that you're looking for Dixie Orlando?"

Ronald looked up quickly toward the kitchen, but Mr. Knight was busy rattling the dishes, and Ronald didn't think he could hear. He answered softly, "Is this Orlando speaking?"

"Naw, this ain't him. All I want to know is do you really want him?" The man's voice was muffled, as though he was trying to disguise it.

"I might," said Ronald cautiously.

"Well, what's it worth to ya if I finger him for you?"

Finger him! Did this character think Ronald wanted Orlando in order to bump him off, rub him out, take him for a ride?

"It's not worth one copper cent," said Ronald firmly. It was just as well to make that clearly understood from the beginning, and they could negotiate from there. Newspapers sometimes find it necessary to pay for information, unfortunately, but not to anonymous telephone callers.

The caller did not seem at all disturbed. "That's what I thought, but I figured it didn't hurt none to try."

"Does that mean you're going to tell me anyway?" asked Ronald, as there was a little pause.

"I might. Let's put it this way. I like to do favors for newspaper guys 'cause I never know when I might need a favor back someday. If I do this for you, can I count on it that you'll do something back for me if maybe sometime I need it?"

"Sure," Ronald agreed quickly, "as long at it's legal. But I don't see how I can arrange it if you won't give your name."

The character thought this over for a while. "I tell you what, let's rig up a little password between us, like them sentries do. Let's see, now, how about 'red jelly beans.' If you ever hear anybody talking about red jelly beans, you'll know it's me and that I got a favor comin'."

"O.K.," Ronald consented, hoping that he would never happen to run into anyone by accident with a particular fondness for red jelly beans.

"Then it's a deal. All right, now, take down this number." Ronald wrote it down quickly. "It's a restaurant, and Orlando will be in there for breakfast at eight thirty tomorrow morning."

"All right, I'll call him then."

"Oh, one more thing, Wilford. Be sure you don't ask for Dixie Orlando and screw everything up. You want to ask for Yankee Pete. You got that? Yankee Pete."

"I got it," Ronald assured him, expressed his thanks, and hung up, feeling that he was in the center of some deep, dark conspiracy. There was no doubt in his mind that he had actually been talking to Dixie

Orlando himself, and he wondered who these characters thought they were kidding, anyway.

CHAPTER 8

Excess Baggage

Although eight thirty was his regular time for arriving at work, Ronald decided not to report in until after he had talked with Orlando. He figured it might involve some chasing around afterward, and he did not know in what direction it might lead him.

His not-too-welcome guest was up early and had breakfast ready for him, another deftly prepared meal, but Ronald's manner was not too gracious. He felt he had a rather good idea what sort of man Mr. Knight was, and didn't intend to give him any encouragement to overstay his welcome.

Of course he couldn't call Orlando from his apartment, so he went to a pay station again. This was a ridiculous situation, not being able to use his own telephone, and he didn't intend to put up with it for very long. His roommate would be back in about a week, but he didn't propose to wait even that long. Jerry was a friendly, understanding young man, but it might take a little explaining as to why it happened that a strange man was occupying his bed.

Ronald dialed the number he had written down, and the call was answered after two rings.

"Costain's Grille." That was a little restaurant on Vincent Street, Ronald recalled.

"Is Yankee Pete there?" asked Ronald in a guarded voice that he felt suited the circumstances, but feeling not a little foolish.

"Who? Oh, sure, sure. Wait a minute." The receiver was placed down, and Ronald heard the same man say, "Dixie, your call's here." If there had been any lingering doubt in Ronald's mind that he might not have been talking with Orlando the evening before, it now vanished completely. Obviously, Orlando had been expecting this call, and Ronald reflected that it was just like a Short Vincent character to ask for money for locating himself. He considered for a moment using the magic words "red jelly beans," but decided against it. On Short Vincent you didn't tell everything you knew.

"Hello?" said Orlando, using a similarly guarded tone.

"This is Ronald Wilford."

"Who?"

"Ronald Wilford."

"You must have the wrong number. I don't know anybody by that name."

Orlando was playing hard to get, and Ronald called upon his reserve of patience.

"I'm a reporter for the *Star.*"

"Oh," said Orlando, as though giving this information careful consideration while still refraining from committing himself.

"I wanted to ask you something about Barry Knight. You know him, don't you?"

"Oh, sure, sure. But look, I can't talk now. Some other time—"

"Sure. How about my coming down to Costain's Grille and talking with you?"

"Here on Short Vincent? You crazy or somethin'? You want to screw everything up—me bein' seen with a newspaper reporter?"

"Well, I've got to see you someplace right away. How about meeting me at the public library?"

"Nix!" said Orlando in a hoarse whisper. "They got guards there— frisk you when you come out."

"The soldiers' and sailors' monument?"

"Nix! Nobody ever goes there. We'd be too conspicuous."

"The terminal, then? Everybody goes there."

"Well, O.K., then. In the lobby, just inside the first door. But you get there first. I can't take a chance on hanging around too long. How soon will you be there?"

"In forty-five minutes sharp," Ronald assured him and hung up.

He had only waited two minutes in the lobby of the terminal before a short man in a slouchy overcoat stepped out of the stream of traffic and addressed him out of the side of his mouth without looking at him. If there is any person more conspicuous in a crowd than a furtive man, Ronald didn't know who it might be.

"Wilford?" he whispered.

"Orlando?" Ronald whispered right back.

"Yeah. Make it fast. What you want to ask me about Knight?"

"I want to know where he is."

"What's the matter, you his baby-sitter or somethin'?"

"I just want to know where he is," said Ronald patiently. "We've got a paper to get out, and need reporters to do it with, so we kind of like to know where they are and what's going on."

"I don't know where he is."

Ronald carefully corrected his terminology. "Can you tell me where he went?"

Orlando's eyes seemed to be fixed on the clock, as though carefully gauging the time until the departure of his train—another pose, Ronald decided, for it wasn't likely Orlando had a train to catch.

"Maybe," he said.

"Well, where did he go?" As Orlando did not attempt to answer, Ronald found his patience snapping, but made an effort to control himself. "Look, you're a friend of his, aren't you?"

"Why, sure I am," said Orlando firmly, looking at Ronald for the first time. "I'd do anything for that guy. He did something for me once. It wasn't a big story—it would have been just an inch of type to him—but it would have ruined me for life. And he didn't use it. Never asked anything of me back, but I'd do anything for him."

"I'm sure of that," Ronald agreed. "Now don't you see that this may be your chance to do something for him? We don't know where he's gone or why. Maybe he's in some kind of danger, and I can help him. Now you're going to tell me, aren't you?"

This seemed to be too long a speech for Orlando to absorb all at once, so he took it a step at a time. "He didn't say anything to me about being in danger."

"No, but are you sure he would tell you something like that?"

"No." Orlando thought it over. "Did he tell you he was in danger?"

"No," Ronald admitted, "but the evidence points that way. If he wanted to quit his job, he would have done that. If he intended to come back soon, he would have told us that. The way it looks, he didn't know whether he was coming back or not." He waited a few moments longer. "Well, haven't you anything to tell me? It had something to do with Walter Desmond, didn't it?"

"Knight'll be awfully sore at me," Orlando stalled.

"How can he get sore when he isn't here?"

Orlando considered this point and apparently decided it rang true. "Say, that's right. But what if he comes back?"

"But he hasn't come back. That's the reason I'm so anxious to find him."

"I don't know for sure where he went—"

"But you know something," Ronald reminded him. "Knight was inquiring for you at the precinct station."

"That was all right," said Orlando quickly. "You can always try the police station if you want to, but don't ever ask after me down on Short Vincent. Knight knew better than that."

"Did he find you that day?"

"What day?" asked Orlando, as though puzzled.

"The Thursday before Christmas."

"Oh, *that* day. No, he didn't find me. But he got my message."

"And what was your message?"

Orlando's eyes narrowed. "You're sure that's all you want out of me—just the message? I don't want Knight to get sore at me."

"Just the message," said Ronald firmly.

The man took a deep breath. "All I told him was: 'Desmond left for Union City,'" and Orlando strolled off, making a great show of comparing his wrist watch with the railroad clock and shaking his head dubiously.

Ronald could almost have smiled. He felt he was beginning to understand a man like Orlando—a man who conducted his business with a great air of mystery to hide the fact that he had no business, who couldn't stand to be frisked because somebody might find out he *didn't* carry a gun, who for all his underworld affectations apparently could walk into a police station and walk right out again—for where else had he found out Ronald was looking for him? And Ronald wondered how many more characters like this there were down on Short Vincent.

Returning to the office, Ronald found that Carole was not at her desk. She had left a note for him, saying she was out tracking down another lead. Ronald went on to the editor's office and found him with a few free minutes. He felt it was necessary to review his progress to date and get the editor's permission for his next step. For Ronald had already decided that he wanted to go on to Union City.

Ronald had only recently come to recognize that a newspaper's reportorial staff is shaped to a considerable extent by the character of its editor. It wasn't that Burnett very often told his men what they ought to write or how they ought to write it. The process was much more subtle than that. If a reporter spent several days on what he thought was a hot story, only to find it reduced to a single paragraph on an inside page when it finally appeared, then he knew that he had considerably exaggerated the importance of the story in his own mind, and wasn't likely to make the same mistake again. And if he found the masterpiece over which he had slaved for hours completely rewritten as it appeared in print, he would carefully compare his own version with the printed version and decide where he had gone wrong. All this was done without a single word from the editor. Ronald had benefited from both types of correction himself.

It took a lot of courage to publish a story that would arouse the anger of an important advertiser, but Burnett had done it many times and would do it again if the circumstances warranted it. "I don't want them to advertise unless it's profitable to them," Ronald had heard him explain, "and it wouldn't be of benefit unless people had come to respect our paper, including the advertising in it." And while Burnett had no objection to giving dignified publicity to worthy persons, organizations, or products, he watched with an eagle eye for the publicity plant. He once tossed out a humorous story Ronald had written, because he recognized the hidden publicity motive that Ronald, in his inexperience, had overlooked; and after getting over his initial disappointment, Ronald respected him all the more for it. Burnett was highly regarded in the newspaper profession, and Ronald counted himself fortunate to be working under such a chief editor and the competent staff associated with him.

Burnett listened without comment until Ronald had finished his summary.

"Knight's father?" he said at last. "You wouldn't expect a fine man like Knight to come from a background like that."

"I don't think his father had very much to do with raising him," Ronald explained, "at least, judging by the way the story was told to me."

"Well, maybe so, maybe so. You haven't given this fellow any money, have you?"

"No."

"Well, see that you don't. It can lead to embarrassing complications. What's your idea of what to do with him now? Are you going to leave him at your place while you go to Union City?"

"No, I don't see how I can do that. I have a roommate to consider, even if I trusted Mr. Knight fully, which I don't."

"You're sure he's not a phony, Wilford?"

"He's probably as phony as they come, but I really do think he's Knight's father. That's why I thought maybe I'd let him come along with me, if he wanted to. That way, even if he was up to something, I could keep an eye on him."

"Well, don't put him on the newspaper expense account, Wilford. It's not the money I'm thinking of, but the principle. Let him suggest it if he wants to go along, and let him figure out how he's going to meet his expenses—that ought to be interesting. After all, if he were really Knight's father he could come to the paper and explain his circumstances, present his credentials, and we'd see what we could do for him. There isn't much we can do as long as he wants to deal on an individual basis."

"O.K.," Ronald agreed. "Another thing, I've got a kid brother lives out near Union City, and I wondered how it would be if I got him to come along, too."

"On the expense account?" asked Burnett quizzically. A highly honest man himself, Burnett liked to pretend that he thought everyone else was dishonest. For him the pose accomplished a useful purpose, for he was always pleased when he found he was wrong, and wasn't disappointed when he found he was right.

"Oh, no," said Ronald in confusion. "That is, he might be of some help to me. He's interested in newspaper work. Besides, he had a broken ankle that tied him up all summer and hampered him during the fall, so it might be a good vacation for him."

"You've sold me, Wilford. And I was only kidding about the expense account. Handle it however you think is fair, depending on whether he really is useful. I imagine I'll be meeting your brother before very long, when he takes over your job—after you've taken over mine."

He spoke jestingly, but Ronald knew there was a more serious purpose underlying his words. This was his way of telling Ronald that he thought the reporter had a good future in the newspaper business.

It had rather been Ronald's hope that he might find the nerve to invite Carole to a movie or play some evening, but now that he was leaving town that day, there wasn't time for that. But at least he could invite her out to lunch, and when she telephoned, he summoned up all his resolution, trying to think what he could say if she turned him down.

"Where are you now, Carole?" he asked of her.

"Oh, way out past South Euclid, miles from anywhere. All on a wild goose chase, and I'm frozen and half starved."

"Why don't you have lunch with me?" asked Ronald, trying to make his voice sound casual. "I'll come out and pick you up, if you want me to."

"The lunch would be fine, Ronald, but don't bother picking me up—I imagine I can make it faster on the bus than you could drive it both ways. You didn't have Short Vincent in mind?"

"Oh, no, you've fully convinced me I ought to stay away from Short Vincent for a while."

"Then let's say the Flambeau at twelve?"

"That sounds good to me," Ronald quickly agreed.

When he met Carole at the restaurant, she explained her errand. "I came across something—a young man who had once threatened Knight's life. But when I came to look him up, I found out he's safely in prison and likely to be there for a good many more years."

"A member of a gang?" asked Ronald alertly. "Maybe someone else might carry out the threat."

"No, I don't think so. He seems to have been a lone worker—young kid from a good family, but gone bad for some reason. I often wonder why it sometimes happens that way."

Ronald smiled. "We reporters must be different from normal people. What you found out this morning is really good news, but that makes it bad news to us because it spoils a story for us."

Then he brought her up to date on his own part in the case, and she expressed once more her distrust of Mr. Knight.

"How did he find where you lived, Ronald? Bratenahl isn't a large place, but it isn't so small that you can go to the first apartment house and find the person you're looking for."

"He said it was more or less by chance."

"And why couldn't he have called you, anyway? Even though you're not listed, he could get the number from the telephone operator, as long as it isn't a private number, or he could have called you at the newspaper office."

"He said he didn't know I worked on the paper. Could he have got my address from the telephone operator?"

"I don't think so—they're pretty careful about giving out addresses in that fashion."

"You may be right, Carole," said Ronald slowly. "It *is* a little strange the way he found me, but I don't think his motive is strange. I think he wanted to talk to me in person instead of over the phone, in order to work on my sympathies a little."

They gave their orders, which were presently filled, and though they talked easily throughout the meal, their conversation did not have very much to do with the strange disappearance of Barry Knight.

Upon returning to his apartment directly after lunch, Ronald explained about his plans to Mr. Knight.

"Is it some clue you've got to my son?" asked Mr. Knight quickly. "If it is, Mr. Wilford, won't you take me with you? I'm so anxious to meet my son—it means more to me than I can say."

Ronald shook his head. "I wouldn't mind, Mr. Knight, except that I simply couldn't afford it. I can't put you on my expense account, and I just couldn't meet your expenses myself. My brother Ted will be coming along, too."

"I've got my railroad pass," Mr. Knight reminded him quickly, "and I think I'll be able to pay all my own expenses. Fact is, I've got a pension check that's sure to come along the first of the month."

"You're sure about that pension check?" asked Ronald keenly.

"'S gospel. Are you going to pack a trunk, or just take a suitcase?"

"I think just one suitcase will be enough. I want to travel light." But I'm already taking along some excess baggage I could just as well do without, he added to himself.

"That's fine. I'll take a suitcase, too. I'll just run down to the shop and get a few little things I need," and he hurried out.

A strange picture of destitution, Ronald thought—yesterday he said he didn't have a dollar, but now that he wanted to travel he appeared to have money once more. It was no great surprise to Ronald—men like Mr. Knight usually have a little more money than they care to admit—and at least his guest's temporary absence gave him a chance to put through a call to Ted.

CHAPTER 9

Ronald and Ted Confer

It was Ted who answered Ronald's call, and he showed surprise as soon as he recognized the voice.

"Ron!" he exclaimed.

"Right on the nose," Ronald replied.

But Ted was all attention, knowing that these were long-distance rates, and that it must have been something rather important for Ronald to call so soon after his visit home.

"Ted, I've got something that's too long to explain over the phone, but what it amounts to is this: how'd you like to take a little trip with me?"

"Why, that sounds great, Ron."

"Sure it won't interfere with your New Year's Eve celebration, or anything like that?"

"Oh, no, we didn't have a party planned, and I'll be getting together with the gang soon, anyway."

"Did Mom have anything planned for the holiday?"

"Well, I think she sort of wanted to go for a visit to Aunt Alice's, but she didn't like the idea of leaving me here alone. This'll all fit in swell."

"All right, then, Ted, listen. I want you to meet me in Union City sometime tomorrow. It's just a small town, so I imagine there'll only be one hotel. If you get there first, and I think you will, you can get us rooms. Make sure you get two bedrooms, because I'm going to have a man with me."

"Hadn't we better get reservations in advance?" said Ted cautiously. "It's the holiday season."

"I've never had any trouble in a small town, Ted. If the hotel's full, they'll probably know of some private family that will take us in. Anyway, I doubt if I have time to confirm a reservation, and rooms or no rooms, I have to be there."

"Then I take the rooms for the week?"

"No, no, I don't know how long we'll be there—not long, I hope."

"What's it all about, Ron?" Ted added hopefully. "Some sort of investigation?"

"Something like that. I'm looking for a man, and I'm not sure he even exists at all. Sound intriguing? I can't go into detail now, but I thought this would give your curiosity a little something to work on. See you tomorrow, then, and I'll tell you all about it."

After hanging up, Ronald set about getting his suitcase packed. He had checked the station just before calling Ted and found that an early evening train would be the best for him. They would take the coach rather than the sleeper, though, for he didn't want to put Mr. Knight to any unnecessary expense. Anyway, he wasn't feeling particularly tired and felt he could get enough shut-eye sitting up in the coach.

He wondered what Ted thought about his call. Probably trying to figure out what it was all about, he decided, for he knew that Ted possessed an unusual share of natural curiosity, along with a special aptitude for solving difficult puzzles. A case like this would be right up Ted's alley, and Ronald was glad he would have someone he could talk the matter over with. Although the two brothers often addressed each other as "muttonhead," they held a high respect for each other's ability. Ted would be bringing a fresh mind to the problem, and perhaps he would be able to recognize some little clue that Ronald had overlooked. Ronald hoped so, for from his viewpoint the case seemed to be bogging down. If he didn't find Barry Knight in Union City, where would he turn next?

When Mr. Knight returned, he had quite a number of purchases. This was the man who just the day before had claimed to be penniless, but he had a glib explanation.

"I stopped down at the railroad branch office, and my check was waiting for me there. They cashed it without any trouble. That ought to tide me over for a week or two."

While his story was possibly true, Ronald couldn't help but wonder how a retired worker on a pension could afford fifty-cent cigars, of which Mr. Knight now appeared to have a lavish supply. At least Ronald was wrong about one thing: Mr. Knight was no sponger. He paid for his own meals on the train, leaving generous tips, and also paid his share of their rooming bill in advance, when they arrived at the hotel. Although everything about him seemed phony, Ronald thought, maybe he really was motivated by a sincere interest in finding his son. Anyway, money wasn't his object, or at least not Ronald's money.

They had arrived in Union City in the middle of the morning. As Ronald had expected, Ted had gotten there before them and had their rooms reserved. The third member of the party was introduced simply as

"Mr. Knight." Ted looked a little puzzled, for he evidently had expected a younger man, but Ronald had no time to explain just then.

"What would you say to an early dinner?" Ronald suggested. "Train meals never fill me up, and maybe we can beat the noonday Sunday crowd."

Ted was very eager to learn more about the mission that had brought them all to Union City and made some reference to it at the table. But Ronald promptly said:

"Oh, let's not talk business at the table. I'd like to forget it for a little while and give my attention to what the menu calls 'home cooking.'"

A shade of disappointment swept across Ted's face, but he was used to Ronald and quick to sense that there were undercurrents here he wasn't aware of. It appeared that for some reason Ronald didn't feel free to talk in front of the third member of the party, and so it would have to wait till they were alone.

When at last the brothers were alone in their room Ronald asked: "What did you think, Ted, when I said I was looking for a man I wasn't sure existed?"

"I know what I thought on the slow train trip here. I thought that Union City seemed to be a pretty difficult place to get to, but as long as a man didn't exist, maybe it was just as good a place not to exist in as any other."

Ronald laughed. Then he went on to explain the situation as clearly as he could. Ted listened with careful attention, and asked a few questions, until he had a pretty fair understanding of the situation.

"And so," Ronald concluded, "it appears to me that this whole affair hinges on whether Walter Desmond is guilty or innocent. Since I don't see how he could be innocent, I don't know why there should be any problem at all."

Though Ted examined the case carefully for any possible loopholes, he had to agree with Ronald that if it wasn't Desmond, it would have to be the proprietor Don. There was no other way to explain how the burglar alarm came to be set. But here Ted was stymied, unable to explain Ronald's objections to such a theory.

"Do you suppose maybe Don was trying to steal Desmond's invention?" Ted speculated.

"I don't think so. He didn't seem to know just what the invention was about, or to be terribly interested. On top of that there wouldn't be a great deal of point in stealing the invention—simply having a model of it wouldn't mean much. I believe Desmond already had a patent applied for at that time. In addition, my impression is that the invention doesn't amount to beans unless Desmond keeps working right along on it, trying to improve it."

"Then if it wasn't the invention," Ted decided, "Don must have had a grudge against Desmond, if Don really did steal his own money."

"Well, maybe, Ted, but I haven't found anything to indicate that there was a grudge. Don seemed willing to forgive and forget the whole thing when I talked to him. But even if there was a secret grudge, maybe of long standing and over something we don't know anything about, we still have to figure out how Don could have stolen the money."

"Maybe he stole it just the way he said. Desmond forgot to set the alarm, and Don came back to check up on him—maybe he made a practice of coming back *every* night. He found the alarm wasn't set, robbed the register, and then set the alarm when he left."

"But if that's so," Ronald argued, "why did he go to so much trouble to tell me about it? And if this was a longstanding grudge and Don was determined to get even, would he have been so patient? How could he be sure that Desmond would *ever* forget to set the alarm? It would take a lot of patience to wait around, maybe months or years, for that to happen, and Don didn't strike me as a particularly patient man. As I explained, setting the alarm was a complicated matter. If it were simply a matter of turning a single key or throwing a bolt, the action could become so automatic that a person might forget to do it, or afterward forget whether he had done it or not. I don't think the same thing would apply so readily to a series of involved actions like this. No, I feel pretty sure that if Don was trying to get even with Desmond, he would have found a more direct, more immediate way."

"Ron," said Ted excitedly as a sudden thought struck him, "maybe Don wouldn't have to wait for Desmond to forget to set the alarm. He could have planned it all for that night. Isn't it possible for a person to think he has done something when he really hasn't?"

"How do you mean?"

"Well, you said that Don liked to fool around with these alarms as a hobby. Then wouldn't he know how to disconnect the alarm somewhere inside, so that Desmond would think he had set the alarm when he really hadn't?"

"Say!" Ronald exclaimed, his eyes lighting up momentarily. "It does explain a reasonable *way* that Desmond could be innocent—provided Don is guilty—and that's the thing that has always stumped me up to now."

Ted was studying his brother's face closely. "But you still don't like it?"

"No, Ted, frankly I don't think we're getting anywhere at all," said Ronald with a sigh. "Your theory is the kind of thing I might think of myself if I were sitting alone in my room. But I've met Don, and I've learned quite a bit about Desmond, and from that point of view it doesn't make very much sense. There's one thing that in my opinion knocks your whole theory out the window. Desmond must have known that his only chance of being acquitted was to pin the blame on Don. And yet at his trial he was very careful not to make the slightest accusation against Don, or to let his attorney suggest such a thing for him. Surely Desmond must have known better than we do what was going on. He didn't think Don did it, and that ought to be good enough for us. No, Desmond must have been guilty. The alarm was set, there was no picture—"

"A picture?" asked Ted.

"Oh, yes, something I didn't mention before. In the newspaper account of the robbery there is one little sentence in which Don is quoted as saying, 'I didn't get a picture of the robber.' That sounded screwy to me, and I thought, either he meant it as sarcasm or else the paper accidentally dropped out a paragraph of explanation. Then just today I realized what it must mean. I'll bet that Don has a secret camera attached to his cash register that will take a picture of anyone who goes into it after hours, or maybe anyone who doesn't press the keys in just the right way. Clever, I guess, but just one more thing to prove Desmond's guilt, and one more reason to wonder why Barry Knight should have been so worried about a guilty man's going to jail."

"That guy Don must be kind of queer," Ted commented.

"I guess you might say that," Ronald agreed. "He admitted to being a screwball. Well, I suppose burglar alarms can be an interesting hobby if you happen to be interested in them, and I suppose there really is a good deal of justification for it in Don's case. Filling stations do seem to get robbed more often than any other type of business enterprise. Even a bar will usually have a number of customers sitting in it constantly. But a filling station operator can be all alone for a while even on a busy night. And the way most stations are lighted up, it's often easy to tell when the proprietor is alone."

He went on, "Don is a factor in this case, and we have to try to see how he fits into the whole picture. I'll put it to you this way: in view of all the trouble in this case, do you really think it is just a small-time robbery, a gas-station proprietor who keeps a barrel of walnut shells in his attic, a guilty man punished, and all this happening so many years ago that it's practically forgotten? Or do you think we're concerned with an important invention, a prominent crime reporter, and a statewide slot-machine racket under Freddie Uglancie?"

"You make it sound pretty important," Ted admitted. "But did you ever think that maybe Don is one of Uglancie's men?"

"Hm, no, I didn't. But I'd be inclined to doubt it. He's a garrulous type—would have told me everything about his business, I think, if I'd hung around longer. Talkative people usually don't have very much to hide, or else they don't do a very good job of it."

The problem of what to do next had to be met. Ronald felt that the first thing was to try to get a glimpse at the hotel register for the day Knight could reasonably have been expected to arrive in town.

"Will the clerk show it to you?" questioned Ted.

"Sometimes they do, sometimes they don't. Anyway, there's nothing lost by trying."

CHAPTER 10

A Spot of Ink

It turned out that the clerk now presiding at the desk was an affable person. When Ronald explained he was trying to learn whether a friend of his had been there on that particular day, the clerk willingly opened the register and shoved it toward him. Ronald saw at once that Knight's name wasn't listed, but he scanned the list just the same to see if any of the persons could be Knight under a different name.

The three married couples could be disregarded, as well as a single girl. That left only two names, and Ronald noticed at once that both men had taken rooms on the main floor, larger display rooms where salesmen could show their samples.

He remarked about the room numbers and commented, "You must get quite a few salesmen in your trade here."

"Oh, yes, quite a number," the clerk agreed. He wasn't very busy just then, and seemed glad to talk.

"What kind of men are they sending out on the road these days?" Ronald inquired. "Ambitious younger men, or steadier older men?"

"We get quite a few of both, but I think there is a trend toward older men. These two men I remember especially. One was a heavy-set fellow with a booming laugh you could hear a block away. The other was an older man, with arthritis in his arm, so that he could hardly carry his sample cases. I felt pretty sorry for him."

So neither of these men could have been Barry Knight. After continuing the light conversation for a minute or two longer, Ronald turned away, feeling disappointed. Knight hadn't come to the hotel, so where else could he have gone? Private homes sometimes had rooms for rent, and if he was going to rent a room, wouldn't he have looked for it in an ad in the local newspaper? Ronald managed to get a copy of the weekly newspaper covering that period and found several rooms listed.

He went up to his room, and after stationing Ted on guard to make sure Mr. Knight didn't come back while he was phoning, he put through the first call. He found the first room had been rented, and the woman explained it had been rented even before the ad had appeared, and she was sorry he had been put to any trouble. At the second number the woman said her room was still vacant, and she seemed pleased to find someone interested. Ronald was very sorry she was going to be disappointed. The third phone rang a long time before a man's angry voice answered. In reply to Ronald's inquiry he said they had changed their minds about renting their room, and he hung up sharply. Well, Sunday afternoon was an inconvenient time to call, but Ronald felt that the matter was so important he had to do it.

It had turned out to be a poor hunch at best, and though he hadn't had much confidence in it, he felt obliged to check it out. Surely Knight wouldn't have rented a private room when he was probably uncertain how long he was going to be there. When Ted suggested that Knight might have stayed with a close friend or relative, another objection held.

"As far as we know, Ted, Knight came here on the trail of Walter Desmond. Wouldn't it be a very odd chance that the trail just happened to lead him to a small town where he had a friend or relative to stay with? No, Knight isn't here at the hotel, and he didn't answer one of the ads in the paper for a private room, and he probably didn't have any acquaintances here. That leads me to doubt very seriously that Knight is in Union City at all."

"What about Walter Desmond?" asked Ted. "Do you think he's here?"

"Well, it is just possible that Desmond came to Union City to stay with friends. But since Knight was looking for Desmond, if Knight isn't here I don't think Desmond is either. About the only possibility I can see is that Desmond is living in a private home, and that Knight found him and moved in, too. But that doesn't sound very probable, since from the looks of things Desmond was anxious to keep away from Knight as much as from anyone else. The way it appears to me, Desmond merely came to Union City because it was the easiest way to get to another place. Knight came here in search of Desmond, quickly found something, and immediately left town. The question is, where did they go from here?"

"I don't think they could have gone farther west," Ted pointed out. "If Desmond was going on west, why stop in Union City at all? He could simply have stayed on the train."

"By the same token it isn't likely he went east, either," Ronald went on. "In that case he would have gotten off the train before it reached Union City."

"Unless he wanted to double back on his tracks to throw off pursuit," suggested Ted.

"Well, that's possible. However, we don't know that Desmond had any idea he was being pursued. We don't know just when Desmond went through Union City, but I imagine it was at least a month ago, and that it took Knight several weeks after that to pick up the trail to Union City. Anyway, if Desmond was afraid of being found and was trying to throw off pursuit, he may have gone anywhere, and our chances of finding him aren't very bright. No, we'll just have to assume that he went through Union City because it was the best way to get where he wanted to go, and try to figure out logically where he went from here."

"I don't think he could have gone south, either," Ted decided. "Turreyville is a railroad junction, with a branch running off southward, so if Desmond wanted to go south he would have got off the train at Turreyville."

"By a process of elimination we have come to the conclusion that Desmond must have gone north." Ronald's forehead furrowed. "I haven't looked at a map. Just what lies north of here anyway? Do you know anything about it?"

"It's sort of open country, I guess, leading off up into the hills. Didn't you notice that big poster down in the lobby? It says: *'HANK HUDSON'S HALF MOON LODGE. HUNTING. WINTER SPORTS.'* And the small print says it's north of here, and there's a regular bus going to it. The clerk told me a little about it, said they were trying to develop a new winter resort up there. Does this help us any?"

"I think it does, Ted," said Ronald, his excitement growing. "A hunting lodge sounds good to me. We really don't know anything about Desmond's business except that he was working on an invention, and a quiet, isolated place might be just what he was looking for."

"We could be wrong about it," said Ted cautiously.

"Yes, we could be," Ronald admitted. "Sometimes all logic points one way, but there's a little loophole, and the loophole turns out to be right. Let's see if we can't think of something to support our theory." He thought it over seriously. "Say, I might have something. When I went through Knight's clothes closet, I noticed that one of the things missing was Knight's loud, flashy hunting jacket. He hardly ever wore it, but I've seen it once or twice. It wasn't very suitable for the city, or even a town, but it would be just the thing for country or sports. Maybe Knight wasn't as much in the dark as we are. Maybe he knew all the time where he was going, and that's why he passed in and out of Union City so quickly. Does this all sound like wishful thinking?"

"Just a little," Ted advised him.

The desk clerk was obliging once more, and not only answered all their questions about Half Moon Lodge, but supplied them with a map. They studied it for several minutes.

"Certainly the closest way for Desmond to get to Half Moon Lodge was through Union City," Ronald pointed out, "so that fits in with our theory so far."

"But there are several small villages on the way to Half Moon Lodge," Ted observed. "Even if Desmond did go north, maybe he stopped off at one of them."

"It could be, but I'm more and more convinced that a small hunting lodge is quite likely. In a small village a stranger stands out too much, but not in a lodge that has a number of guests. I'd say the odds favored good old Hank Hudson, and I'm willing to bet on it. Ted, as far as I'm concerned you've earned your salt on this trip already."

Inquiry told them that there was only one bus each day to Half Moon Lodge, and that it left at nine in the morning. Whether they liked it or not, they would have to stay over in Union City for the night, which meant a dull New Year's Eve.

"Think you'd care for a movie?" asked Ronald, without much enthusiasm. "I suppose they'll be jam-packed, though."

"I believe there's only one movie in town, and I've seen the picture already."

"Any good?"

"Not good enough to fight through a crowd."

At that point a knock sounded on the door, and when Ronald opened it, he found an employee of the hotel standing there.

"The party is just beginning downstairs. Would you care to join the other guests?"

"Isn't it a private party?" Ronald questioned.

"Oh, no, guests of the hotel are entirely welcome. Won't you come down?"

"Glad to!" Ronald and Ted answered.

As they got ready to go downstairs, Ted looked for his white shirt which was at the bottom of his suitcase where it was less likely to get mussed. It had been painstakingly folded and put away by his mother, and he took it out carefully. As he unbuttoned it down the front, he suddenly gave a gasp of disappointment.

"What's troubling you, son?" Ronald inquired.

"Look—on my shirt. A big splotch of ink on the collar. I can't wear this shirt tonight, that's certain. I wonder how it happened?"

CHAPTER 11

Stubbed Toes

"Don't you have another shirt you can wear?" asked Ronald.

"Oh, yes. I guess Mom put in two white shirts for me instead of just one. But I still can't understand it, Ron. Mom's such a careful packer."

"It's from your fountain pen, isn't it? It must have jogged loose on the train and then leaked out on your shirt."

"It's from the fountain pen, all right," Ted agreed slowly. "I was looking for it this morning, but decided I must have forgotten to put it out for Mom to pack."

"Well, it's only a spot. Mom'll have some way of getting it out. Now let's hurry up and get downstairs."

"It isn't just the spot, Ron. There was something else happened this morning. I brought along an envelope with newspaper stories for the paper I wanted you to look over. Margaret Lake wrote a story about the surprise Christmas party at the children's home, and I'm almost positive that when I put them away that story was on top. But when I came to take them out of the envelope, it was stuck away in the middle."

Ronald was all attention. "What did you think happened?"

"Well, of course, Mom packed my suitcase, and though I know she wouldn't snoop, she just might have looked into the envelope to make sure it was something I really wanted to take along. But I don't know—along with this spot on the shirt, it just doesn't sound like Mom at all. I think someone went through my suitcase on the train!"

"Did anyone have the opportunity?" Ronald questioned him closely.

"Yes, there was a pretty good chance. Not on the bus—I had my suitcase on the rack overhead, just as I did on the train. But on the train I left my seat once. The porter had told me there was a magazine and refreshment stand up front, and I was getting kind of bored with so many stops and decided I might as well pick up a sports magazine."

"Could it have been the porter or one of the railroad employees?"

"Not the porter. He was up front by the stand. There wasn't any conductor on the train, or, if so, I didn't see him. They took our tickets when we got on."

"How many passengers were there?"

"There were just the three of us—this man who got on at Logansview when I did, and another man who was sound asleep the whole trip. The three cars ahead were all empty. I suppose they were intended for the early commuter traffic out of Union City." He stopped for a moment. "What do you think, Ron?"

"So you believe it was this man who got on at Logansview? It would have been pretty risky. The other passenger might have awakened, or you might have returned sooner than he expected."

"I don't think he would have had to worry about the other passenger—he looked pretty far out of this world. And I don't think he would have had to worry much about me, either. He was sitting on the aisle just a few seats behind me. He could have hauled down my suitcase and put it on the seat beside him, and looked through it while he kept an eye out for me. He could have seen me coming a long way off—I wasn't hurrying any—and put the suitcase back without my seeing him."

"There's nothing missing out of your case?"

"I can't be sure just what Mom packed, but I don't think so—not anything valuable, anyway."

"It's hard to figure, Ted. It's quite possible your fountain pen became loose in the suitcase, and it's also possible that Mom looked to see what was in the envelope and accidentally dropped your papers, and that's how they became disarranged. But suppose this man did go through your case. He must have been just an ordinary sneak thief. I don't see how it could have had anything to do with the case we're investigating. We didn't decide till yesterday that you were coming along, and it would have been hard for anyone to get on to you in that short time."

Because Ronald seemed to dismiss the matter as of little consequence, Ted found himself almost convinced. They were dressed by that time, and after a quick glance in the mirror, they went downstairs. The main reception room was gaily decorated, and a small orchestra was already playing.

If they had expected everyone else in the room to be a stranger to them, they were mistaken in one respect, for they soon discovered that Mr. Knight had also come downstairs and joined the party. He was clean-shaven with his hair slicked back, and he was wearing the latest style of clip-on bow tie. Altogether he presented a remarkably different appearance from the bedraggled old man who had played upon Ronald's sympathies.

Long after midnight when they had gone to their room again, Ted emerged from the bathroom looking puzzled. "Just stubbed my toe over the suitcase Mr. Knight left in the bathroom."

"Occupational hazard," said Ronald carelessly, for it wasn't his toe.

"Something queer just the same," said Ted in a low voice. "When I bumped the suitcase one of the initials came off."

"So what? They've been on there so long, it's a wonder they didn't fall off before this."

"That's just it, Ron. I don't think so. If the initials were put on when the suitcase was new, you'd think the leather under the initials would look newer, wouldn't you? But this doesn't. You can't even see where the initial went on, and the leather there looks just as battered as the rest of it. It looks to me as though those initials were just pasted on lately."

"Mm," said Ronald, who was busy at the moment going through his own suitcase. "Say, something queer here. If I didn't know better I'd say somebody's been through my suitcase, too. You weren't rummaging through here, were you, Ted?"

"Sure not. Don't you think I like the way my head fastens on?"

"Well, it surely looks like somebody's been through here, and not very carefully. I never leave my shaver cord tangled up this way, and it's never occurred to me to put socks in my shirt pocket. What's going on anyway, Ted? What have we got that other people want?"

"I'm sure I haven't got anything that would do that man on the train any good. But that man isn't registered here at the hotel, so he can't be the one who did this. Who do you think it was, anyway?"

"Mr. Knight, maybe."

"But he was downstairs at the party most of the time."

"He went down after we did. He'd have had time. Or maybe it was some of the help here. Ted, you've got me thinking about that initial. I'm going to take a look."

He did, and returned to the room with a thoughtful look on his face. "You're right, Ted, it does look as though those initials were just added lately. But why, why?"

He sat down on the edge of the bed, his forehead rested in his arms. Ted watched him for a moment, then said:

"It doesn't look very good, does it?"

"I'll say it doesn't," Ronald agreed with reluctance. "It looks like I've been taken in as the prize sap of the old year. Those initials are just one of the casual little details you absorb without thinking, just one of the small things that helped convince me this man was Barry Knight's father. Now it looks like those initials were just glued on to make an impression on me. This time I've been so wrong it isn't funny. I should have guessed, though. Both Burnett and Carole warned me about this man, but I thought I knew more than they did."

"Carole?" asked Ted.

"Carole Curtis," said Ronald. "You've heard me mention her."

"Oh, sure," said Ted, grinning.

"Of course it wasn't the initials so much," Ronald went on. "The real thing that convinced me was that I was so sure Carole and I were the only ones who knew anything about Barry Knight's background in Imperial. Mr. Knight's story fitted in with as much as we knew. I'm sorry about your sore toe, Ted, but it looks to me as if I've stubbed my toe over this a lot worse than you did, and I'm going to have to come up with something big to clear myself."

"Who do you think Mr. Knight really is?" Ted questioned.

"He isn't Barry Knight's father. I'd be willing to wager almost anything on that right now."

He had been up and pacing around the room, but now he sat down on the bed again and motioned Ted beside him.

"Let's keep our voices down to make sure this so-called Mr. Knight doesn't overhear. No, I don't know who Mr. Knight is, and I really don't think it matters very much. The important thing is, what is he after?"

"He's trying to find Barry Knight, isn't he?"

"Exactly. Since my main mission is to find Barry Knight, and he managed to get himself invited along, that must be what he wants, too. Now who besides myself is interested in finding Barry Knight? I can think of only one person—Freddie Uglancie. He invited me to help him, and I refused, so this must be his next step. I feel nearly positive that Mr. Knight was hired by Uglancie to help him find Barry Knight."

"They surely went to a lot of trouble, didn't they?"

"They sure did, and not only that, but they had to work fast. They must have known about that Imperial angle, and they must have had a pretty good idea I hadn't found out very much down there. Therefore they were able to make up a convincing story. They did that, all right. Look how careful they were with the details. They supplied Mr. Knight with a railroad pass, and I'll wager now that he never worked a day on the railroad in his life. Then there were the initials, and the story about his check, and this long, elaborate story about Barry Knight's relations with his father.

"Do you realize where all this leaves us? Probably not a word that Mr. Knight told us was true. We still don't have a single thing about Barry Knight except a vague feeling that he was once connected in Imperial, and that there was a gasoline station robbery there. We still don't know the real story about that letter the minister wrote for him. Barry Knight is as much a mystery as ever, and I'm beginning to believe my first hunch was right—Barry Knight is a person who doesn't exist."

"I was puzzled about that," said Ted seriously. "You hinted over the phone that we were looking for a man who didn't exist, and then when I got here you introduced me to his father. If he didn't exist, how could he have a father?"

"I'm convinced Mr. Knight is here for only one purpose. He is reporting to Uglancie everything we do, everything that might give Uglancie any hint about where Barry Knight is. I believe Barry Knight was just about ready to blow the lid off Uglancie's slot-machine racket—or at least Uglancie is afraid he is—and that Uglancie is determined to find him at all costs."

"And then what?" asked Ted carefully.

"Yes, and then what? Oh, I've been a prize sucker in more ways than one. Maybe I'm doing Barry Knight a great disservice by trying to find him at all. At least I didn't do him any good when I helped Uglancie's men to pick up his trail."

"What about that man on the train?" Ted reminded him. "You think he's another one of Uglancie's men?"

"Yes, Ted, you've about convinced me about your man on the train. I didn't see how they could have picked you up so soon, but then I didn't see how they got on to the Imperial business, either. It wouldn't have been so hard in your case. Mr. Knight left my rooms just as soon as I told him about our trip, and he must have phoned Uglancie immediately, who put his own man on to you. He must have already had a man out in this area, and it wasn't hard for him to pick you up. And of course it's clear now what he wanted—any hint we might offer about where Barry Knight is hiding himself."

"What are we going to do now, Ron?" asked Ted, feeling his excitement mounting. Big things were happening, and he felt squarely in the middle of them. "You think we can give Mr. Knight the slip in the morning?"

"No, Ted," said Ronald slowly, "I don't think I want to play it that way. He already knows what bus we're taking and where we're heading. He's found out the most important things from us, so it's too late to worry about that. He knows Barry Knight is probably hiding at Half Moon Lodge—for his own sake I hope he isn't, though I'm very much afraid he is. But we have got one advantage. We know Mr. Knight is a phony, but they don't know we know he's a phony. That's our trump card, and we'd better keep it hidden until we're ready to take the trick."

CHAPTER 12

North to Half Moon Lodge

They were up in plenty of time to catch their bus. The sun came up brightly, and their high spirits lingered from the party, so that Ronald was willing to cast a more forgiving light on Mr. Knight.

"He's a scoundrel, all right, but he isn't quite the sort of scoundrel I thought. In my opinion a father who neglects or abandons his children is just about the lowest form of animal life. But he probably never did that, no matter how much he tried to make me believe he did. And think what a good actor he had to be. Of course if he was going to pretend to be Barry Knight's father, then he had to invent some story about how the two had been separated for so long. Otherwise, I would have had too many questions he wouldn't have been able to answer. Just the same I had questions, and the answers rolled right off his tongue as smoothly as you please. It was a superb job of acting, and I hope he's been well paid for it."

"You think that's all he's in it for—for money?"

"Oh, I imagine so—that's what most people are after. I don't think he's one of Uglancie's men—he doesn't seem quite the type to me. I imagine Uglancie hired him for this job, to try to find out what he could from us about the whereabouts of Barry Knight. That explains another thing, too. When he first came to me he acted as though he were broke, and now I believe that he really was broke. I think that this money he's been throwing around was a down payment from Uglancie, after he'd managed to work his way into my confidence. He collected it when he was out supposedly getting his pension check cashed."

"Even so, Ron, Uglancie couldn't be sure you'd really believe he was Mr. Knight."

"That's true, and I think that perhaps Uglancie didn't care too much. It was just a long shot that might come through or might not, and if it didn't, he'd try something else. First I refused to help him find Barry Knight; then he hired this man to pretend to be Barry's father, and if that didn't work, he would have gone on to a more drastic step."

"Such as what?" asked Ted, his eyes narrowing.

"I imagine it would have involved having me followed, making sure of everywhere I went, every step I took. Of course it wasn't necessary after they managed to get this fellow on the inside."

"Then you believe he searched your suitcase last night, too?"

"Yes, Ted, I do."

"What do you think he expected to find?"

"That's just it, Ted. I don't think he expected to find anything at all. He had plenty of time to search through my things before this, and he could have done it in a much more careful fashion. For these very reasons he may have thought I wouldn't suspect him, but would perhaps blame it on some of the help here, who would certainly have passkeys."

"This doesn't make much sense, Ron. What good did it do to have him search your suitcase?"

"I imagine he did it under orders. You remember last night that we were talking a little bit loudly when you discovered that spot on your shirt. I imagine he overheard a good deal of what was said, and reported back to these people he's working with. When they learned you were suspicious about that man on the train, they ordered him to do something to divert your suspicions. While they didn't necessarily want us to grow suspicious of Mr. Knight, still the man on the train was of more importance to them. That's why I think Mr. Knight is rapidly coming to the end of the road as far as his usefulness to Uglancie is concerned, and that's the very reason why I think we have more to gain by keeping him with us. I hardly think they had any hope he could keep up the masquerade indefinitely."

Mr. Knight joined them just a short time before they were due to leave for the bus. They had all skipped breakfast, but no one minded, for they had eaten so well in the early morning hours.

"That was a night," said Mr. Knight, shaking his head in reminiscence. "I didn't know these old legs had that much ginger in them any more. A little bit stiff this morning, but it was worth it, every minute."

"Yes, they certainly treated us like royalty," Ronald agreed, "especially considering that we're strangers here." He went on, looking directly at Mr. Knight: "Or are you acquainted here in town? I thought I heard you using your phone last night." Ronald saw no harm in a shot in the dark.

"You did?" asked Mr. Knight in surprise. He appeared to recollect. "Oh, I remember now. I called down once to room service. That must have been what you heard."

Ronald considered this for the feeble support it gave to his theory. But that Mr. Knight had been hired by Uglancie hardly seemed to be a theory. He was virtually ready to accept it as proven fact. That Mr. Knight was Barry's father was ridiculous on the face of it, and he would never have accepted it for a minute if he'd been more alert.

At the station Ronald sent a telegram to the paper to inform them of his destination. Then the trip to Half Moon Lodge was begun without further incident.

When they left Union City, the ground was covered with a light layer of snow, which had been worn thin by recurrent drizzles during the past couple of days as the mercury inched above the freezing point. But as they progressed farther up into the hills, the snow lay deeper, and neither the rain nor advancing temperatures had made much impression on it. Though far from the soot of the city, it still gave the impression of having lain on the ground for a long time.

"We had a couple of real deep snows a little before Christmas," the bus driver explained, "and most of it's still with us. That's all to the good. It helped out the vacation trade up at Hank Hudson's Lodge—that's where you're going, ain't it? Yep, a good deep snow is just the thing for winter sports, but this rain the last couple of days didn't help any. Drove everybody indoors, I understand."

"Is it a very big place?" Ronald questioned him. "The reason I ask is that we didn't bother to make reservations."

"Oh, there'll be plenty of room," the driver assured them. "Rooms filled up, they pull out a few extra mattresses in the main room. That's the kind of place Hank's is. But he won't be full up now. This last week was his big week, and after this there won't be much doin' except on weekends. I just carted a load of customers away Sunday night, and there haven't been many coming in to replace them. You won't need reservations. Fact is, Hank's is one place you can't just call up for a reservation."

"Why not?" Ronald inquired.

"No telephone," the driver chuckled. "That's one of the attractions of the place, I guess. Lots of businessmen want to get away for a few days where their offices can't reach them. Got electric lights, though—run their own generator. You'll be comfortable enough up at Hank's."

The part about no telephone sounded like an unusual concession to the rustic atmosphere, and it both pleased and disturbed Ronald— pleased him because it made the lodge sound like a rather isolated place that might have attracted Walter Desmond; disturbed him because his office might have trouble getting in touch with him if they wished to.

The traffic was light, but the near-freezing temperatures made the road slick in spots, so the driver did not try to make time. This was a small, independent bus line, and apparently no one worried very much about keeping to a rigid schedule. There were other passengers, but these got on and off at the several small villages through which they passed, most of them giving the driver a familiar "Howdy." It seemed that Ronald and his two companions were the only travelers who intended to go all the way up to the lodge.

At one of their stopovers, as noon approached, Ronald suggested they might as well have their dinner. The driver thought this a fine idea, and ate with them. What this did to his schedule they couldn't guess, but Ronald imagined that this was a one-man bus company, with their driver-owner representing the whole works.

The lodge was a mile and three quarters beyond the last village, and the bus brought them right to the door. As this was as far as the bus went, Ted pointed out when he was able to get Ronald's private ear, it was a cinch that Walter Desmond hadn't gone much farther north than this.

"Trip back every afternoon at five o'clock," the driver reminded them in parting, and added a word that they felt inclined to doubt: "Sharp!"

They had had no clear idea of what they expected, but the lodge was a nicely designed affair, set in colorful surroundings. Fir trees were numerous, their boughs heavily weighted with the wet snow, and a few not-too-steep hills nearby suggested some pleasant skiing was available when they wanted it. There were no other buildings in the area, however, except for a few small shacks in the rear which were apparently associated with the lodge.

The indoors was about what the exterior had led them to expect, comfortable quarters with a backwoods atmosphere. A huge fire blazed in the fireplace, but this must have been part of the effect, for steam radiators spoke of central heating. A huge bearskin hanging upon the wall behind the desk immediately attracted the eye, as did a number of mounted trophies suggestive of big-game hunting. Only one guest was in evidence, sitting reading in a chair, so that the lodge was hardly up to its capacity of an estimated twenty-five or thirty guests.

Ronald registered for the three of them, then struck up an easy conversation with the man at the desk, who introduced himself as Hank Hudson.

"Then you're not crowded here just now?" Ronald queried.

"Oh, no, not just now, though last week was a good one for us. The first day of the New Year is an awkward one—either people got where they wanted to go before that, or else they're on their way home. That's Mr. Lane sitting in the chair over there—you'll soon get acquainted with him. And we have a couple of other guests who are outdoors just now, and some others who are up in their rooms getting ready to leave on the late afternoon bus. You probably won't have a chance to meet them.

But I'm expecting another load up tomorrow, so you'll have plenty of companionship."

Ronald nodded toward the trophies. "Are there really bears and moose around here?"

"Well, I sure wouldn't like to say no." The proprietor shook his head mysteriously, then as Ronald smiled, he added more seriously, "No fooling, there are some deer around here, and if my guests have hopes of bagging something bigger, who am I to discourage them?" He was looking over their baggage, and noticed the absence of rifles. "Think you might want to try your luck? I've got rifles to loan, if you do."

"No, thanks, I guess it's a little out of my line." He nodded toward Ted. "My brother's a skiing enthusiast, though. Think you can fix him up?"

"Oh, sure, I've got skiing equipment available, too—or almost anything else you might want."

"How are the hills?" asked Ted.

"Some of them are all right, though this thaw has sure been a business-killer. You an expert?"

"No, just a beginner."

"Then you'll be able to find a practice hill, all right. It depends a good deal on how the sun hits."

He came around the desk to help them with their bags. "Will you men be wanting something to eat? You're a little late for dinner, but my wife can fix you something if you want it."

"I don't think so." Ronald looked to Ted and Mr. Knight for their agreement. "We ate coming up."

"Then supper's at six, and you can meet the other guests then. Meanwhile, if there's anything you want, just let me or my wife know. I won't say ring, because there aren't any buzzers."

Having settled down in their room, Ronald asked of Ted, "Well, what do you feel like doing this afternoon?"

"What do you want to do?" Ted countered. "After all, we're here on business, aren't we?"

"I suppose we are. Even though this is a holiday, we'd better try to get some results soon to justify the swindle sheet. The truth is, though, that I haven't had much sleep the last two nights, and I don't see much chance of accomplishing anything until I've seen who else is here at supper."

"You're expecting Barry Knight?" Ted demanded.

"You never can tell. But if it turns out we're on a wild-goose chase, the only thing that will cheer me up is remembering that we've led Freddie Uglancie off the trail, too. I can see you don't care much for the idea of a nap, so why don't you try out one of the skiing hills? There's no reason you shouldn't get in as much fun as you can, and it'll help me if you sort of scout around and get the lay of the land a little."

Ted thought this was a good idea, and left the room a few minutes later to pick up a pair of skis and poles, along with some well-meant advice from Hank Hudson. Although Ronald fell asleep soon afterward, some inner clockwork awakened him in time for the next step on his schedule.

He was anxious to get a look at the guests who were just departing, on the chance that Barry Knight or Walter Desmond might be among them. This task proved simple enough. Barry Knight certainly was not among those leaving, and since the men appeared to be a group all well acquainted with each other, it wasn't likely Desmond was among them, either. Well, Ronald would just have to wait for suppertime to get a look at the other guests.

Back in the reception room, Mr. Lane was still reading in a chair, and Ronald sat down near him. Thereupon Mr. Lane promptly dropped his magazine and appeared eager for conversation. They exchanged names and home towns, but if Ronald was a little worried that Mr. Lane might prove too prying, he could have saved himself the trouble. Mr. Lane was more interested in talking than in listening.

He talked on and on, adding a good many details of his home life that Ronald wasn't the least bit interested in. But not having anything else to do just then, Ronald appeared to be attentive, and Mr. Lane rambled happily on. Finally he leaned forward confidentially.

"Would you think it terrible of me if I made a confession? My name really isn't Lane at all, and I'm not from Baltimore as I said. I didn't mean to deceive anyone except my secretary; I would have told any of the guests if they'd asked me, but no one seemed interested. My real name's Payne, and I'm from Detroit."

Ronald started. Detroit, the Motor City—did that mean anything? He had never forgotten that the invention Walter Desmond was working on was a new kind of car battery. Hadn't Desmond's trip up here had something to do with his invention? That was the best theory Ronald had been able to work out, and a gentleman from Detroit certainly fitted into the picture.

CHAPTER 13

The Three Guests

Ted came in, fresh and enthusiastic from his skiing, but without very much to report.

"There isn't much around here, Ron. No one lives any closer than the village. But there are a few deserted cabins where somebody could hole up for a while if they wanted to. They're not in sight from here, but a man told me about them."

"Who were you talking to?" Ronald asked.

"He didn't give his name, but he's staying here at the lodge, so you'll meet him at supper. He talks rather queerly—a lot of big words, and everything. He sounds like a college professor to me."

"Professor Villinger," Ronald remarked. "I picked up his name from the register. Did you see anyone else?"

"Not to talk to. Somebody else came in, a big, heavy man."

"Carrying a rifle?"

"No. Ought he to be?"

"Not necessarily," said Ronald, with a deep breath that suggested exasperation, "but I never expected to see so many persons at a hunting lodge who weren't interested in hunting. Mr. Payne, who goes under the name of Mr. Lane, doesn't seem to be interested in anything except sitting and reading in the reception room and talking to everybody who comes along. He's the kind of talker who's hard to break away from, unless you want to be openly rude to him—probably has bored everyone stiff so they know enough to keep out of his reach. Also, he comes from Detroit."

"Is that bad?" Ted demanded.

"I wouldn't know, except that all along I've had a secret hunch that somebody from Detroit would be getting mixed up in this affair. It fits in rather neatly with Walter Desmond's invention and his reason for coming up here."

"Maybe Desmond only came up for a vacation, too," Ted suggested. "I imagine he could use it, after being in prison for six years."

"I suppose so," Ronald agreed, "except that he must have been out of prison for a month or so before he came. But six years—that's an odd period of time. Does it mean anything to you, Ted?"

"No, I don't think so. Should it?"

"Well, I've done quite a bit of police-court work, and to me six years just stands out like a sore thumb every time I hear it. Did you ever hear of the 'statute of limitations'?"

"I guess I've heard of it," said Ted vaguely, "but I don't know enough about it to explain it."

"It's a law stating that a man must be accused of a crime within a certain period of time. I haven't studied law, but I imagine that the time may vary with different states and for different crimes, and certain serious crimes like murder and espionage may be exempt, while of course it doesn't apply to fugitives. But in our state, and I think a good many other states, the period is six years. Unless a man is charged with the crime within six years of the time it is committed, he is free ever afterward even if it can be definitely pinned on him."

"That sounds rather generous," Ted decided.

"It's one of the fundamentals of our freedom. For instance, what would you do if out of a clear blue sky somebody accused you of committing a crime twenty years ago?"

"I think I'd have a pretty good alibi," Ted grinned. "I wasn't born yet."

"No, but I think you know what I mean. You'd have a tough time proving your case, getting witnesses together on your behalf, and so on. Besides, I think there's an underlying philosophy back of this law. If a man has managed to live down an earlier offense, created a good life for himself without getting into further trouble, he ought to be given the benefit of any doubt. Now let's see how this applies to Desmond. Here we have a man who *wanted* to stay in prison for six years, which just happens to be the same period of time as the statute of limitations."

"I don't get it, Ron," said Ted frankly.

"Well, let's suppose this man had committed *two* crimes, a lesser one and a greater one, and let's suppose that he was caught and convicted of the smaller crime while no one suspected the bigger one. Now applying for a parole would mean reopening his case again, and he might have been very anxious that his case should not be reopened until the statute of limitations had run out. As soon as the six years was up, Desmond *did* apply for a parole and was promptly released."

"You really think that's maybe what happened?" asked Ted, his eyes squinting into a frown. "I thought we were up here because of a chance that Desmond might have been innocent."

"I don't know, Ted. My theory doesn't quite fit in with what I've been able to learn about Desmond. Everybody who knew him seems to have held him in high regard, even the man he robbed. But when a man stays in prison longer than he has to, it does suggest some sort of cover-up, doesn't it?"

Ted snapped his fingers. "Something else I forgot to tell you. Do you know what Mr. Knight was doing this afternoon?"

"I thought he was taking a nap in his room."

"No, he wasn't. I saw him walking down to the village. It was tough walking, too, for an older man. I felt kind of sorry for him, but it must have been important."

"Must have been," Ronald agreed. "I thought he was acting pretty tired this morning. The lodge has almost everything he could want, including cigars. Besides, I'm sure he could have got a ride down from Hank if he'd asked for it."

"What do you think he wanted, then?"

"What do *you* think?" asked Ronald pointedly.

"It must have been the telephone, then. He wanted to get in touch with somebody."

"That's just what I think," said Ronald with emphasis.

The brothers were up in their room, preparatory to going down to supper. As they were about to leave the room, Ronald said:

"Something to keep in mind, Ted. We still don't know whether Walter Desmond is here at the lodge, but if he is it's possible he's using a different name. We don't know what he looks like, but keep your ears open to see if you can come up with anything that suggests one of the guests is really Desmond."

In the dining room, as the guests arrived, Hank performed all the necessary introductions. Besides Ronald, Ted, and Mr. Knight, there appeared to be only three other guests: Mr. Lane, Professor Villinger, and the heavy man Ted had seen whose name was given as Mr. Bogus. The newcomers were also introduced to Mrs. Hudson, who was busy serving the meal and so did not sit with them.

"A little cozier group than we've been used to this past week," said Hank as they took their seats, and he repeated his expectation of more guests the next day, as though that would be an added attraction.

The conversation opened up as the meal was begun. Mr. Lane spoke pleasantly to the other men, but apparently they had learned the hard way not to give him too much encouragement. In addition, Mr. Bogus was the kind who liked to talk, too. Although he had "big business" written all over him, he spoke mostly about birds, and Ronald supposed it was quite natural for a businessman on vacation to show greater interest in his hobby than in his work.

"Saw a scarlet tanager today," said Mr. Bogus, casting a triumphant look around the table. "What do you think of that?"

The others hardly knew what to think, not knowing whether scarlet tanagers were rare or common, and only the professor had an opinion.

"Are you sure it was a scarlet tanager? They're a migrating bird."

"No doubt about it whatever," said Mr. Bogus in his booming voice. "I got the glasses squarely on him, and you couldn't miss that flaming red body and the black wings."

"The female is rather greenish the year round," said the professor mildly, "and the male's coat becomes more greenish in winter, too. The youngsters are very dull." He didn't seem to be an arguing type of man, but merely liked to be accurate. However, not wishing to provoke a dispute between himself and Mr. Bogus, he referred the matter to their host. "What do you think, Hank?"

This placed the proprietor in the difficult position of siding with one guest against another, and he tried to compromise. "I believe the male is somewhat splotched with red even in winter, and although I've never seen a scarlet tanager here in winter, I suppose even in a migrating group there will be a few individuals who stay behind."

"This one did," said Mr. Bogus decidedly, and he wasn't the sort of man who could be easily contradicted.

Hank led the conversation away from birds and back to food. Everyone joined in an enthusiastic appreciation of their meal, which was everything that could be expected.

Mr. Knight also was a congenial talker and had an interesting story to tell about how he had worked his passage across seas on a tramp steamer. It was the sort of story that was rather endless, and could easily be built up if his listeners' response justified it, or brought to a speedy conclusion when interest lagged. This time he had a responsive audience, and sensing it, he carried on to some length. But at last he had no other choice than to bring the freighter limping safely into port after a disastrous storm.

By chance the professor had been seated between Ronald and Ted, and although he was a little harder to draw out, he didn't mind talking about himself when he had been sufficiently encouraged.

"I'm up here on a college grant," he explained. "They're interested in making a study of avalanches, and this seemed a good place for a season's study."

"I told him he's wasting his time here," Hank broke in, for the topic appeared to be an unwelcome one to him. "We've never had any trouble here with snowslides," and Ronald could not help but notice that he avoided the use of the more terrifying word, "avalanches."

"No," said Professor Villinger, "but this has been an unusual year, with especially heavy snowfall, and now this thaw. Anyway, the university is just as interested in finding out why we *don't* have avalanches on certain hills. There are many different types of natural catastrophes that can strike people. Earthquakes are something we can hardly predict at all; storms, volcanic action, and floods can be predicted with a certain degree of accuracy; but with tidal waves and avalanches we ought to be able to approach almost complete accuracy."

"I shouldn't have thought that predicting an avalanche was such a difficult thing," Ronald remarked. "It's merely a question of getting too much snow and then it starts to slide, isn't it?"

"If that were so, nobody except a few foolhardy people would ever get caught in an avalanche. No, it's an enormously complicated subject, which may be the reason it attracts me. For one thing there are different types of slides. A loose snowslide takes on the shape of a developing fan. If the snow is dry, it slides partly as a big cloud, and you are just as likely to be suffocated as you are to be buried. A wet loose snowslide is more destructive. However, it usually happens directly after the snow has piled up through snowfall or wind, so that it's not much of a surprise. A slab snowslide is altogether different. The dangerous situation may have been building up for months, until something triggers a sudden break, and it lets go."

"What sort of trigger?" Ted questioned.

"It can be a loud noise, or a light fall of new snow, even a skier cutting across a slope. Of course none of these things would cause an avalanche unless the slope was already dangerous, and that's the sort of thing I'm supposed to determine. It depends on so many factors, such as the character and moisture content of the snow when it fell, the angle of slope, the cohesion between the ground and the snow, and between the different layers of snow, the rate of settlement, temperature, wind, and so on. The whole battle is between the weight of the snow which is pulling it down, and cohesion which is holding it up. During a thaw your cohesion is lessening, and the snow may begin to slide."

"Don't you do anything interesting during the summer?" asked Hank, a little bitterly.

"Oh, yes, I correlate my results from the winter before, and make my plans for the next winter," said the professor with a smile.

"Is there any danger on the hills around here?" Ronald inquired.

"Not at this very moment, if my calculations are correct." He acted as though he would just as soon be buried under a snowslide as to live to find out his calculations were in error. "But I'm watching the hills at the mouth of Lonely Valley. They may give me some trouble if this thaw continues. I may have to take steps."

"What steps can you take?" Ted asked. "You can't prevent an avalanche, can you?"

"Not prevent it, exactly. The simplest thing would be for everyone to stay away from the dangerous hills, but people being what they are, it is often safer to start the avalanches ourselves by means of explosions, rather than to wait for nature to do it."

"You said our hills are safe now, didn't you?" Hank persisted.

"Certainly, unless I've made an error." He spoke with resolution, as if this were sufficient assurance for him and ought to be enough for the others.

Mr. Bogus, who had been silent for a long time for him, now spoke up. "I can imagine a scientist blowing up a city, and his last coherent thought would be: 'Oops! A pinch too much thorium.'"

"From what I've seen of scientists," said Mr. Lane, "they always claim to be saving lives, and if they lose a few doing it, they don't mind, as long as it isn't their own."

There was a little laugh at the professor's expense, but he was unperturbed. "I have the equipment and the necessary permission from the state for conducting a few experiments on controlled avalanches. I may undertake them a little later."

"After the winter tourist season is over, I hope," said Hank, rather disturbed.

"Yes, unless I find it necessary beforehand." It was hard to tell if he was completely serious or merely choosing to string his host along.

After supper they settled down in the reception room. As part of the rustic atmosphere, there was no radio or television set, but it was a pleasant place to read or talk quietly. However, fearing that they might become a little bored, Hank finally suggested that he run off some of his home movies, and the guests were all agreeable.

It turned out that he was a good photographer, and his colorful movies represented some good amateur work, if perhaps a little long for strangers. Ronald congratulated him afterward, and Hank's good humor appeared restored. After all, it was easy to understand why he disliked the talk about avalanches, which might have a serious effect on his trade, and it was a little inconsiderate of the professor to pursue the subject when he realized how much he was bothering his host. Devotion to science may be a good thing, but it shouldn't override all social considerations.

"Your uncle's quite a talker, isn't he?" said Hank to Ronald, who was momentarily puzzled that Hank should have mistaken Mr. Knight for a relative, but did not bother to deny the relationship. "I'd sort of like to have him up here next holiday season at my expense, just to create atmosphere for the other guests. Do you think he might feel insulted if I offered him a proposition like that?"

"I think it would take a good deal more than that to insult him," said Ronald with a laugh.

The group broke up early, and Mr. Knight left for his room about the same time they did.

"That was quite a yarn you spun," Ronald said to him. "But I thought you had worked on the railroad all your life. I didn't know you'd been on a tramp steamer."

"Well, of course it never really happened to me," Mr. Knight admitted, "although it was a true story—mostly. But people appreciate a story more if you make it sound like a personal experience."

They left him at his door, parting with a friendly exchange of good nights, and went on farther down the hall to their own room.

"Well, what do you think, Ted?" said Ronald, sprawling out on the bed for a few minutes. "Look the three guests over: a scientist who's anxious to set off some dynamite explosions as though he were playing with a new toy; a businessman who'd like to make us think his only interest is birds; and Mr. Lane-Payne, who pretends to be hiding out from his secretary and admittedly comes from Detroit. Which of these three men, if any, is Walter Desmond?"

"Bogus sounds like a phony name to me," Ted observed.

"It's certainly unusual, to say the least, although I've learned not to be too surprised at anybody's last name. But it does sound just like the sort of name somebody might make up. Mr. Bogus may have a high degree of everyday, hard-rock commonsense, but I don't think he's a particularly imaginative person. He might invent a name like this and think he is being very subtle, without realizing how obvious he is."

"Doesn't anybody ever use his right name?" Ted wondered. "I never before heard of so many people traveling under aliases."

"It does look that way, Ted," Ronald agreed with a smile. "Hank ought to have a double-entry register listing everybody's real name and the name they're going under. Mr. Lane-Payne of Detroit is another character I'm wondering about."

"There must be about half a million men in Detroit, Ron, and probably not more than a dozen of them would be interested in Walter Desmond's invention."

"Yes, I suppose so, and another thing is that he was so open about admitting he came from Detroit and was using a false name. That hardly makes him sound very suspicious, unless it was just his way of covering up. And then there's our scientist friend. He has the technical background and he just might be interested in an invention. He's a complex man who could have much more behind him than we realize. However, putting them all together, I must admit that none of these three men quite matches the picture of Walter Desmond I had been building up in my mind. I didn't picture him as quite as well educated as the professor, or as aggressive as Mr. Bogus, or as gabby and flighty as Mr. Lane-Payne. I wonder if we're off on a wrong tack altogether?"

"What about the other guest?" asked Ted.

"What other guest?" said Ronald, straightening up and staring at Ted with quick interest.

"Just after she got finished serving us, I saw Mrs. Hudson carrying a tray toward the stairs, and I'm sure as shootin' it wasn't for the cat."

CHAPTER 14

The Northeast Room

"A tray of food," Ronald mused. "I suppose it's possible they have another guest we don't know anything about. Still, it could be some employee of theirs who is sick. This is a pretty big place for Hank and his wife, to run all by themselves."

"But I think they do run it by themselves when they're as empty as this," Ted maintained. "Something Hank said to me when I was talking to him about skiing made me think that they depend on part-time help from the village when they're full up. He said he didn't have anyone just then who could help me out with my skiing, because they'd let their temporary help go."

"Well, you could be right, Ted. Stay here awhile. I want to scout around a little."

He returned to their room in less than ten minutes. "I've looked the situation over as well as I can, Ted. Discounting the rooms where I know guests are staying, and the empty rooms that are standing with the doors ajar, there's one room left over. It could be the room at the end of the side corridor, the northeast room, only it's still fairly early, and I didn't see any light under the door."

"The northeast room," Ted pondered as he tried to remember.

"Why, do you know something about it?"

"Just a minute until I get my directions straight. I looked the place over from the outside, and I noticed there was an outside stairway leading up to one of the rooms. Yes, that would be the northeast room. I remember now."

"Well, so our mysterious guest has a private stairway, apparently so he can get in and out without being disturbed. That certainly doesn't sound very much like a sick person, now does it? And if they did have a sick guest, wouldn't Hank have mentioned it to us? Another thing, I happened to run into Mr. Lane-Payne, and I asked him casually if there had been a sick guest. He looked very vague about it, and thought I must be referring to one of the men who had just left. It looks very much to me as though this guest suddenly got sick just when we arrived."

"Then who do you think it is?" Ted demanded. "I know we came here hoping to find both Walter Desmond and Barry Knight, and we haven't found either of them. Which one do you think it is?"

"Well, if it is either one of them," said Ronald thoughtfully, "I imagine it would be Barry. Remember Walter Desmond doesn't know us from Adam, unless Barry has told him about us. Even then he wouldn't have any reason to hide from us, especially if he was using a false name, since we don't know what he looks like."

"He might think you had a picture of him," Ted reminded him.

"That's so, I might, except that the Imperial paper covering the trial didn't print his picture. I don't know whether the warden at the prison would have showed me his picture or not, but anyway I didn't ask. Regardless of that, I still think it's more likely to be Barry than it is Desmond. If Desmond was here, I think Barry would have found him. If Desmond isn't here, Barry may have come along on a false scent the way we did. I can imagine Desmond and Barry Knight together, or I can imagine Barry here alone, but I can't imagine Desmond here alone."

"Maybe they're both in the same room," suggested Ted.

"Well, I suppose that's possible, too, although not very likely if Barry was pursuing Desmond and Desmond was trying to elude him."

Ronald considered the matter very carefully as Ted watched him in silence. Finally, as Ronald seemed to have made up his mind, Ted said:

"What have you decided to do, Ron?"

"I wonder, Ted, if the time hasn't come for a showdown with Barry. This trying to run away from everything is beginning to seem pretty silly. If I've managed to find him, then that means Uglancie's men will be on to him soon as well. I think I ought to warn him about that. He may need our help, and it's about time that we let him know we're on his side."

"That's all very nice, but how are you going about it?"

"In the simplest, most direct way I can think of. I'll simply go over there and knock on his door. I don't think he'd be foolish enough to pretend not to recognize me, or to try to get rid of me after I've come this far to find him. If I can just get him to talk frankly with me, we'll be able to figure out what the score is."

"What if it isn't Barry Knight?"

"If it's a stranger I'll simply make my apologies and withdraw, and just where that'll leave us I don't know. But I'm going to play along that it's Barry till I find out otherwise. There's only one thing that bothers me, Ted. I don't want our phony Mr. Knight to get on to what I'm doing. He's probably carried everything back to Uglancie already, and that's something I want to put a stop to right now. I'll tell you, our room's between his room and the northeast room, so I don't think he can follow me without passing this door. While I'm gone I want you to listen very carefully just inside the door for anyone coming along the corridor. If someone comes, you open the door as though by accident and engage him in loud conversation so I'll hear you. Or if it should be Mr. Knight, you can ask him in, tell him I want him to wait for me because I've got something important to talk to him about. Whatever you do, don't let him go near the northeast room."

Ted was agreeable and took up his station, prepared to execute his mission faithfully. Meanwhile, Ronald turned down the dimly lighted corridor and into the near blackness of the shorter side corridor. No doubt he could have turned on a light, had he bothered to hunt for the switch, but he felt that that was too likely to attract attention to him. So he half felt his way along the wall until he reached the door of the northeast room. There was still no light beneath the door, but he decided not to let that deter him.

He knocked lightly on the door, then listened carefully for a response. There was no sound from within, not even a telltale rustle. Was the occupant asleep, or was he simply determined to ignore any intrusion? Ronald rapped once more, a little louder, then waited once more, still without results. He decided to try one last time and knocked as loudly as he dared without disturbing the guests in the nearest occupied rooms. There was no answer.

He tried the doorknob gently, and to his surprise it turned. His pulse began to pick up tempo. If he was caught entering a room occupied by a stranger, he was likely to find himself in hot water. If it was Barry Knight, of course it wouldn't matter, and he had already decided to play it that way. He pushed the door wide open and went in.

It was nearly black inside, and he could see very little. He closed the door gently behind him and groped for the switch. He found it presently and turned on the light. There was no one in the room—fortune had favored him that far—but he hadn't found Barry Knight either. The bed was mussed, and the supper dishes were neatly stacked upon the tray. The room had been occupied, all right, but that outside staircase had fulfilled its purpose.

Some personal effects were scattered about, indicating that the occupant intended to return. By examining them, Ronald might have been able to determine whether they belonged to Barry Knight, but he felt that if he were caught he would be placed in too compromising a position. He silently withdrew, turned out the light, and closed the door carefully behind him. Then he made his way back to his own room.

Ted was still on guard but had nothing to report. There had been no disturbance of any kind at his end, but he was surprised to see Ronald back so soon. Ronald recounted his failure, and Ted commiserated with him in silence.

"But if it was Barry, where do you suppose he was going at this time of night?" Ronald pondered.

"Maybe to the village to telephone," suggested Ted, recalling the phony Mr. Knight's similar mission in the afternoon.

"Well, could be," said Ronald, disgruntled. "I keep forgetting this confounded lodge doesn't have a telephone. I never appreciated the value of telephone service so much as today. The simple life is all right, but this is getting ridiculous. Oh, by the way, Ted, the room had only a single bed, so I don't think there were two men in there. Well, I guess that's it for tonight, Ted. Tomorrow's another day."

Ted was an early riser, and was out with his skis before breakfast. When he returned, to find Ronald getting up, he had something to report.

"I think whoever's in the northeast room has come back. I went past that way deliberately, and I thought I heard a little noise inside, and then when I went outside I found some fresh footprints by the back stairs."

"How fresh?" asked Ronald with a yawn.

"They looked to me as if they'd just been made this morning. It didn't snow during the night, but there was some wind, and the older prints are a little blown over."

"Did you try to see where they led?"

"I couldn't. They joined a path a little farther on, and were too confused to follow."

"Well, if our friend Barry Knight went out to telephone, it must have been a long conversation. How's breakfast coming? Until I've had my coffee I don't care what happened to Barry or Desmond or General Custer."

"You've got about ten minutes," Ted informed him, consulting his wrist watch. "I guess almost everybody's downstairs already except Mr. Knight."

"He wouldn't be," said Ronald in some disgust. "I'm getting tired of calling him Mr. Knight when we know he isn't, but I think we'd better keep up the pretense even between ourselves."

"Are you going to try to see Barry Knight this morning?" Ted wanted to know.

"I doubt if I'll get a chance. I don't dare try it if anybody's around, and I think there will be. I've got a feeling that Mr. Knight will be dogging my every step, all in the friendliest, most innocent fashion, afraid that we might find out something that he doesn't know. I think I'll wait until tonight and try again, and if that doesn't do it I'll have to think of something else."

"If it is Barry Knight in that room, do you think anybody knows about him?"

"Hank Hudson and his wife would have to know, of course. Since they're covering up for him, they must have a pretty good idea what's going on. Hold on a minute, though. If it is Barry Knight, Hank doesn't know him by that name. He thought Mr. Knight was our uncle and spoke to me about inviting him up here next winter. Surely if he had a Mr. Knight downstairs, and another Mr. Knight upstairs, he would have put two and two together."

"Unless he was playing it smart and was trying to worm a little extra information out of you."

"There's always another angle, isn't there? But no, I don't think so. If he thought there was skullduggery going on, his best bet would be to sit tight and say nothing. If he was in Barry Knight's confidence, he would play it the way Barry wanted, and I don't think Barry would want him to say anything that might arouse suspicion. The way I see it, if Barry Knight is in the northeast room, he's there under a different name."

"If there is such a person as Barry Knight," said Ted with a grin.

When they went outside after breakfast, the fresh air felt good, and the smell of firs brought a welcome tang to their nostrils. The wet snow was heavy and clinging, though, and made for slow going. They walked westward toward the village, until it came into view just beyond a low rim of hills. They did not go all the way, however, but retraced their steps, taking their time.

"There's something you can do if you want to, Ted. You mentioned that there were a number of abandoned cabins around here. If you go out with your skis today, why don't you try to see how many cabins you can find within a reasonable distance? We know that the lodger in the northeast room spent the night somewhere, and I'd like to have some idea where."

"Then you don't think he went down to the village?"

"I don't think so. I suppose he could have taken a room for the night down there, but why should he when he had a room at the lodge? If he had some little mission in the village, he could have completed it and come back. I've a feeling that he went somewhere else, and for some reason more important than just a whim."

Ronald had been correct about Mr. Knight dogging his trail. After they left the lodge, the man had come out and kept them in view, even though the heavy walking was more of an ordeal to him. Very likely he was relieved when they turned back, and was all smiles when he came up to them as they approached the lodge.

"Just getting a breath of air myself," he told them. "You appreciate the clear, cool air right out of the hills, after being cooped up in dirty, smoky cities."

However, he didn't appreciate the clear air enough to stay out in it after they went inside. He was right behind them as they went into the cloakroom just inside the rear entrance. Ronald had come in to stay, but Ted was there only long enough to pick up his skis before proceeding on his mission.

"I want to be here when the new guests arrive," Ronald said to him in a low voice when they had a moment alone together. "There's no telling when that blasted Toonerville Trolley of a bus will get here, and I want to see if Mr. Knight's telephone call produces any new visitors for us."

Ted smiled, having learned from long experience that inactivity was always an irritation to his older brother.

"O.K., Ron, I'll see what I can do about the cabins. I'd rather be out on the open hills than sitting around waiting all morning. Is that what you're going to do?"

"I suppose so," said Ronald resignedly. "I'll be listening to Mr. Knight ramble, and he'll be watching me, and I'll be watching him, and neither of us will get anywhere—at least until the bus comes. I don't know why I'm putting so much confidence in that bus, but I've got a hunch it's going to bring some new development—if it ever gets here."

"Maybe I'll be back by that time, noon at the latest," Ted promised. "So long—see you."

"Don't break your neck," said Ronald gloomily.

Ronald's prophecy proved accurate, and Mr. Knight did attach himself closely to him throughout most of the morning. Fortunately the bus was early that day, the passengers apparently less willing to put up with the driver's frequent delays. Ted also had returned just before the bus's arrival, and was at Ronald's side when the new guests came in. At sight of the first guest, he clutched Ronald's arm.

"That man," he said in a whisper, making sure that Mr. Knight, who was standing a little distance away, could not overhear, "is the same man who was on the train with me, the one I think went through my suitcase."

"Which man do you mean?"

"The heavier man."

"He's the one? Well, I know who the other man is, the tall one with the slight mustache. He's Marv Lister, the gossip columnist, and I can tell you it would take something pretty big to bring him up here."

CHAPTER 15

Mr. Bogus and the Birds

The newcomers crossed the room directly to the desk. Though they passed only a few feet away, they did not look at Ronald or his brother, but Ronald—perhaps because he was looking for it—thought they exchanged quick glances with Mr. Knight.

Hank left the desk to show them up to their rooms. A few minutes later Mr. Knight, his thoughts seemingly occupied with something far, far away, also strolled out of the room. Being already convinced that Mr. Knight and the man on the train were both tied up with Uglancie, Ronald hardly needed this further proof of his theory. The gossip columnist, Marv Lister, was something new in the picture, though, and Ronald wondered just how he fitted in.

When Hank returned to the desk, Ronald sauntered over to him.

"Wasn't that Marv Lister, the newspaper columnist?" he inquired.

"Yes," Hank answered, with seeming pride that his lodge might be due for some publicity, "he's the one. You two ought to get acquainted. You're a newspaperman yourself, aren't you?"

Since Ronald had already dropped some hint to this effect, he was quick to admit it. "I've already met Mr. Lister, but he appears to have forgotten. As long as that's the way it is, I'd prefer not to be remembered to him."

The conversation continued for a few minutes longer, but either Hank didn't know why Marv Lister was there, or else he wasn't saying. Ronald felt inclined to believe that the coming of the famous columnist was as much of a surprise to Hank as it was to him.

"Hope he puts a little item in his column about this place," said Hank eagerly. "A little thing like that would shoot trade way up, maybe make me add on a new wing."

"Provided he said something good," Ronald reminded him.

"Oh, it would have to be good, wouldn't it?" said Hank anxiously. "I've got a nice little place here—good food, clean, pleasant surroundings, and Lister's going to get the best service you ever heard of. This is one of the best locations I know of for winter sports when it gets fully developed. Ought to have an artificial ice pond to use when the weather betrays us, and we could put up a toboggan slide, maybe even a ski lift."

"And a little better transportation to get here," Ronald put in.

"Well, yes, it is a little awkward. We're not readily accessible by air, which cuts down our business considerably. Maybe the railroad would build a spur, or we could put on a few extra busses. We don't get much private automobile trade because most people don't like to drive this far in winter. I always thought our isolation was a point in our favor, but of course things would be different if we went big time."

All this because of the possibility of getting a small item in a syndicated column, Ronald thought, and decided that Hank had a pretty good thing the way it was, and would be better advised to leave it that way. If the big-time operators came in, he was likely to find himself squeezed out.

"I didn't recognize the other man with Lister. May I ask his name?"

"It's Marty Grossen. He didn't state his business, but I figured he was Lister's assistant."

More likely a bodyguard to judge by appearances, Ronald thought. He was a burly sort of fellow who looked as if he never read a newspaper beyond the comics and the sports.

Returning to the bench where Ted was sitting, Ronald said, "It was Lister, of course, and the man with him is named Marty Grossen. I don't think there's any question that he's one of Uglancie's men."

"I wonder if he wasn't afraid I'd recognize him as the man on the train?"

"Maybe he didn't know; maybe he didn't care. Coming out in the open as they're doing now, it looks to me like they're ready to blow things wide open."

"Does Marv Lister know you?"

"He should. At least twice we've been present in the same group, once at a political meeting and once at a reception for members of the press. I think he recognized me, all right, even though I represent the opposition paper. Besides which, Mr. Knight must have told him all about me. Since he isn't trying to hide his own identity, he must have decided that I'm not important enough to notice."

Ronald smarted a little under the rebuff, for he knew that Lister was at the top of the newspaper heap while he himself was close to the bottom. Not that he envied Lister's reputation. Quite the contrary. It was the sort of reputation he hoped never to acquire for himself.

"We can't be sure that Lister and Grossen are working together," said Ted carefully. "Maybe they only became acquainted on the way up here."

"No, Ted, they look to me like two of a kind. Besides, Lister must be up here on a big story, and we've got a pretty good idea what that story is. I'm just beginning to get an inkling of what they've got in mind."

Ted was giving Ronald his fullest attention.

"I remember something Uglancie said to me," Ronald began slowly. "He said something about when somebody hits him, he hits back. As I understand it, he never wants to start trouble, but if somebody hits him with a fist, he hits back with a fist; if somebody shoots at him with a gun, he shoots back with a gun. In other words, he gives back exactly what he gets.

"Now what did he get from Barry Knight? Some unfavorable newspaper publicity. So what would be his best method of striking back? Why not with some unfavorable newspaper publicity? You could see what that would do to Barry. If Barry intended an exposure, then Uglancie would expose him instead. If he could succeed in getting Barry discredited in the eyes of the public, that would automatically help to discredit anything that Barry might write about him. It's the old rule of chess, that counterattack is often the best defense. Uglancie intends to counterattack and pull no punches, and he wants to use Lister's gossip column as his method of attack.

"I don't know whether you know very much about Lister's methods, but his reputation in newspaper circles is rather unsavory. It's said of him that he will publish anything in his column for a price. I've heard enough to believe it's true that Lister accepts pay for putting certain items in his column. Look how anxious Hank is to get some little mention in Lister's column, and how much good he thinks it would do him. Believe me, there are some people who would pay plenty to get a write-up there, and I can wager that Lister's price comes high.

"Of course, there has to be some limitation. Anything Lister writes has to be true, or at least basically true, although he may add his own insinuations. If he printed things that weren't true, he'd soon find himself so bogged down in libel suits that he'd have to close up shop. Truth alone isn't a complete defense against a libel suit, but it's a pretty good defense, and I think that as long as what he says is true he's willing to take a chance.

"And that's very much what I think Uglancie has hired him to do: to print the truth about Barry Knight."

"And what is the truth about Barry Knight?" Ted questioned.

"I don't know," said Ronald, looking very worried. "That's the thing that bothers me. I still don't know whether there is such a person as Barry Knight, and certainly he's gone to some pains to cover up certain items in his background. Besides that, I don't know what Barry Knight is doing up here. Whatever it is, I hope it isn't anything that's going to sound too disreputable when it gets splashed all over Lister's column, which is almost certain to happen. That was what Barry Knight was afraid of all the time, and the thing that made him leave town perhaps for good."

"What do you want me to do?" asked Ted.

Ronald consulted his watch. "It's just about time for dinner now. Afterward, if you're still keen about some skiing, I can't think of anything better for you to do than to follow up that mission I gave you this morning. I'd like to know where all the cabins around here are located, whether anyone's living in them, whether they look as if someone had been living in them recently, or if they *could* be lived in if necessary."

"Something cooking?" asked Ted knowingly.

"At least it's on the fire, but I don't know when it'll come to a boil. How are you doing on the skiing? How many maneuvers have you mastered?"

"Oh, quite a few, but mostly the ones I invented myself."

All the guests except the lodger in the northeast room were present at the dinner table. Lister's voice was loud, and he generally managed to drown out less vigorous competition. He didn't mind letting everybody know who he was, assumed that they recognized the name as a matter of course, and went on to tell of some of his experiences. Whether he knew it or not—and he probably did—the whole theme of his talk was what a big, important person Marv Lister was.

None of his remarks were addressed to Ronald, nor did he offer any indication of recognition. His companion, Marty Grossen, meanwhile, had hardly a word for anyone, but sat sullenly and ill at ease. Mr. Knight, too, was unusually quiet, apparently afraid of betraying by any sign that he was acquainted with Lister and Grossen.

After the meal was over, Ronald engaged in a pleasant little game, or rather two little games. Mr. Knight was as anxious as usual to stay close to Ronald and keep track of what he was doing. But with Lister and Grossen the game was just the opposite, and they seemed eager to avoid Ronald. When he came into the room, they found an excuse soon afterward to leave, and after this had happened several times in succession there could be no doubt it was intentional. Actually, Ronald couldn't help but wonder what they were up to, too, but decided it was probably nothing just then. Everybody was marking time, though for just what development Ronald didn't know. His own plan remained to try to arrange a private interview with Barry Knight, but that was beginning to seem more difficult now that he had three men to watch out for instead of just one.

Hank seemed much less cheerful the next time Ronald talked to him. Ronald guessed that Hank had been talking to Barry Knight, who had probably told him the newspaper columnist wasn't up here just for a vacation. Not only had Hank's air castles collapsed with a bang, but he realized that he now faced more difficult problems than he did before. However, Ronald was fully convinced that Hank would be on his and Barry's side if any trouble should develop, and that was a matter for satisfaction.

It was shortly after the afternoon supply wagon had come up from the village that Hank called Ronald over to his desk.

"I just got word, Wilford, that there's a long-distance call waiting for you down at the village."

"O.K., thanks. Where do I take it?"

"In the drugstore. There's only one. You can't miss it."

Ronald hesitated. Since he felt sure he and Hank were on the same side, mightn't it be a good thing to confide in each other? He felt that both he and Hank had only part of the picture, but if they had a better idea of what was going on maybe they could work something out between them. It was hard to believe that Barry Knight's situation was completely hopeless. Might not Hank at least be willing to arrange a secret interview between Ronald and Barry? Apparently Barry had been avoiding Ronald as much as he had anyone, but now that he was faced with the greater danger posed by the presence of Lister and Grossen, mightn't he decide to turn to Ronald for help?

On the other hand, it was probable that Hank was carrying out Barry's orders and wouldn't feel free to do anything without permission from Barry. Maybe it would be better not to precipitate anything until Barry had made up his mind. The fact that Ronald didn't know what name Barry was using was another obstacle. Anyway, there was that call at the village, which just might offer some new angle on the case. As Ronald still debated, Lister came into the room, and the opportunity was lost for the present.

Just as Ronald was getting ready to leave, Ted arrived back with his report.

"There doesn't appear to be anything between here and the village to the west, Ron. So I started south, and then worked over toward the east. I found about six or seven cabins and marked them all out on a little map. Nobody was living in them, but a couple of them looked to be in pretty good shape. Somebody could be staying there if he wanted to, though I can't be sure that is the case."

"Fine, Ted. That's just what I wanted to know."

"Another thing, Ron. I came across Mr. Bogus out on one of his bird walks. He started out to the east, but I came across his trail later. As soon as he was out of sight of the lodge, he immediately switched to the north. It looked to me like he was hiking along, too, not just wandering around looking for birds. I remember that yesterday when I saw him come back he came from the north, too."

"What's north of here, Ted?"

"Lonely Valley, I guess—the place Professor Villinger was talking about. I didn't check up that way for cabins, but I can go out again if you want me to."

"No, Ted, I don't think that will be necessary. You've done a good job already, and besides I've got something else you can do for me. Are you feeling very tired?"

"No, I've just got my second wind."

"Sure your ankle's not bothering you?" asked Ronald, studying him closely.

"Nary a twinge."

"Well, then, Ted, here's what I'd like you to do, if you would. There's a long-distance call waiting for me down at the drugstore in the village. I'm pretty sure it's the newspaper calling, and I wonder if you'd like to go down and take it for me. I imagine you could make much better time on your skis than I could hoofing it, but that's not the important thing. I'd just as soon not give these fellows around here any indication that anything's in the wind. They're used to your going out skiing, but they'd all be alerted if I went down. The status quo is rather precarious here, and I don't want to do anything to upset it."

"Sure, Ron," Ted agreed quickly. "Any messages?"

"No, I don't think so. Tell them anything they want to know except about some of our guesses. I don't want them coming back to haunt me. One thing, watch out that no one listens in on the telephone call."

Ted was off again in a few minutes. The sun shone intermittently, and with the temperature still ranging slightly above freezing, the thaw was continuing slowly. However, he had no trouble finding enough glazed, firm snow to support him, and made a good run down to the village.

Taking off his skis and standing them against the wall, he went into the drugstore. Inquiring for a long-distance call for Ronald Wilford, he was told:

"It's been waiting an hour. You can take it in the first booth over there."

Ted went into the booth and closed the door after him. No one in the drugstore could overhear him, and there was no switchboard girl, either, other than the one in the telephone exchange building. If she should be listening in, there wasn't anything he could do about it.

He put the receiver to his ear and dialed the operator. "I'm inquiring about a long-distance call for Ronald Wilford."

"Is this Ronald Wilford?" she asked.

"No, this is Ted Wilford, his brother, and I'm ready to take the call for him."

"Just a moment and I will see if the other party will accept you." There was a various clicking of instruments until the operator said, "On your call to Ronald Wilford, will you accept Ted Wilford instead?"

"That will be satisfactory," a woman's voice said.

"Then go ahead with your call, please."

"Hello, Ted," said a pleasant voice.

"Hello. This is Ted Wilford."

"This is Carole Curtis from the office of the *Twilight Star.* How's the school newspaper going, Ted?"

He knew she wasn't inquiring about the school newspaper at long-distance rates, not without a purpose. And her purpose must be to make sure this was really Ted.

"We're pretty busy putting together our graduation number. Eight pages, with a class picture and all."

Apparently satisfied, Carole went on, "Ted, I've come across something I think Ronald will want to know. First let me ask you, did he ever study French?"

"He had two years in high school."

"I thought so. Now how do you spell the name of this man who was arrested for robbing the gas station?"

"Why, I suppose it's d-a-y-m-o-n."

"Yes, that's about what I thought. Ronald's been giving it the French pronunciation, Day-*mon.* That's why my eye skipped over it half a dozen times without catching it. Do you know about the graduation program?"

"Yes."

"Well, you tell Ronald that the name Lawrence Desmond appears on that graduation program. Have you got that? Lawrence Desmond."

"Yes, I have it."

"That's all I wanted, then. Making any progress?"

"Some."

"Have you found Barry Knight yet?"

"That would be a little hard to say, Carole. The situation is pretty complicated. I think Ron will have something to report to you pretty soon."

"Three minutes," the operator interrupted.

"Good-by, Ted," said Carole.

"Good-by, Carole," he responded.

He left the store and slowly put on his skis, wondering just what effect this new development was going to have on the case.

CHAPTER 16

Deep-laid Plans

"So Lawrence Desmond graduated from Imperial High School in the class that Barry Knight said he graduated with," said Ronald, pacing restlessly about their room after Ted had brought him the news. "The funny thing about it is that I have never actually looked at that graduation program myself since the name of Walter Desmond first came into this case. What did Carole think about it?"

"I don't think she thought very much of your French," said Ted with a smile.

"Well, if this is so, it certainly sets me up as the prize stupe of the New Year as well as the old. I should have checked that program myself, and even if I didn't do that I should have been able to work it out by logic. All the time I had this most obvious, most important fact staring me in the face, and I never quite fitted it in."

"What fact?" asked Ted.

"Why, I don't think there's any doubt that Barry Knight is Walter Desmond's son. It's hard to say just why I wasn't able to figure that out from the beginning. I know I picked up the idea that this phony Mr. Knight was Barry's father, and hung on to it even after Carole and Burnett warned me against it. But all that came later. Right from the beginning there was some reason why I couldn't connect up Barry Knight with Walter Desmond. The idea was just blocked out of my mind."

He continued to pace about, then suddenly pounded his fist into his hand. "Say, now I know what it was. The newspaper accounts of the robbery and trial never mentioned that Desmond had a son. A big-city paper certainly would have done that, even though they would have soft-pedaled it a little to preserve the son's reputation. My trouble is that I'm a big-shot city reporter, and I've forgotten my small-town background. A little country newspaper wouldn't bother printing such an obvious fact that was already known to everybody anyhow.

"Well, I've certainly goofed this whole case right from the beginning. I overlooked the biggest clue in the whole affair, fell for the story of our phony Mr. Knight, put Uglancie's men on to Barry's trail—I wonder if there're any other mistakes I could have made if I'd really tried?"

"You did a lot of things right, too," said Ted loyally. "Your job was to find Barry Knight, and if he's the man in the northeast room, then you certainly did that, all right. Uglancie with all his big organization couldn't find him, but you did it. And you were the first one who got on to that Imperial business and linked up Barry Knight with the gas-station robbery and Walter Desmond. You can't blame yourself because every piece of the puzzle didn't fit into place the first time."

"I suppose that's right," said Ronald, a little soothed, "especially when so many of the pieces were missing. Well, the important thing is that I don't make any more mistakes from now on. Let's try to reconstruct the whole case from the beginning and see where it leaves us."

He sat down on the edge of the bed, and Ted did the same.

"First," Ronald began, "we have Lawrence Desmond living with his father in the small town of Imperial. I suppose he had no mother, since she has never entered the case. The father worked at a gas station, while he tried to perfect his invention on the side. He stole three hundred dollars from the cash register, possibly because he needed it for his invention. Because of an odd circumstance—which was either a boy's prank or a second attempt at burglary the same night—a broken window attracted attention at the station. The robbery was discovered earlier than Desmond had planned, and because of this he was easily convicted and sent to prison. He did not put up much of a defense at his trial, and I think now that was because he wanted to spare his son's feelings just as much as he could.

"The son went on to finish high school, then went to the minister and asked for a letter of recommendation, which the minister wrote for him. However, there was a different name on the letter. Let's see if we can figure that out. I've been carrying that letter around in my wallet where I was sure our snoopy friend couldn't get his hands on it."

He took the letter from his wallet and smoothed it out on his lap, as Ted watched over his shoulder. Ronald looked puzzled for a few moments, then suddenly he laughed.

"Look at that, Ted—the name Barry. What do you think about it?"

"It's been erased," Ted observed.

"That's it. The first letter has been erased, but because there were several other erasures in the letter I never paid any attention. I don't think there's any question but that the minister used the name Larry, and that later the boy changed it to Barry."

"Kind of a sneaky thing to do," was Ted's opinion.

"We can't be too harsh. We don't know just what problems the boy was facing. I imagine that he asked for the letter and received it, in good faith. It was only afterward when he was mulling over his troubles that he began to think there would be some advantage in changing his name, and the minister's use of the friendly, informal nickname gave him an easy opportunity to do it. But that I was so slow in figuring out what happened is just another of my blunders on this case. Are you keeping track of them, Ted?"

"I lost count long ago," said Ted, who wasn't averse to teasing his brother a little when the circumstances justified it.

"Anyway, the boy came to the *Twilight Star* and got a job under the name Barry Knight. At this time, we can't be sure just what his feelings were toward his father, whether he resented him, felt sorry for him, or felt that his father had been unjustly convicted. We have no proof that Barry ever kept in contact with his father directly, but we do know that he was in close touch through Dixie Orlando. Whether Desmond actually knew anything about his son's circumstances at this time we can't say. Maybe he didn't know for sure, but was able to put a few things together.

"Six years passed, during which Barry Knight rose in the newspaper world, while his father languished in prison and refused to apply for a parole. When the six years was up, two things happened at about the same time. One was that Barry Knight was about ready to close in on Freddie Uglancie, while Uglancie was searching about desperately for something he could pin on Barry Knight. The second thing was that Desmond was released from prison. Now Desmond did not look up his son when he got out of prison. Just why, we can't be certain—maybe he was afraid his prison record would react unfavorably upon his son's reputation. Anyway, he went away, and Barry followed him, the trail eventually leading all of us here to Half Moon Lodge.

"Now I don't think there's much doubt that Barry Knight was actually afraid of what Uglancie might find out—his whole manner of leaving suggests that. Exactly what did Barry have to be afraid of? Was it his father's jail sentence? Well, that wasn't so good, but then it wasn't so bad, either. His crime wasn't what we would call a major one, and anyway our society has made enough progress so that we don't hold a son responsible for what his father may have done. However, the water runs a little deeper than that, for we know that there was another crime in Desmond's background. Just what it was we don't know, but it may have been something more serious, something that would explain why he was given such a severe sentence for the gas-station robbery.

"So we know of two crimes on the father's record. That certainly would have reflected on Barry Knight if the matter came to light, but

I still don't think it would have been enough to damage his reputation very seriously. So we must ask ourselves a question: Was this all? Or was there more crime in Desmond's background, possibly another serious crime that made him willing to stay in prison until the statute of limitations had expired? And have we reached the end even yet, or is Desmond's presence here—if he really is here—based upon some new, bigger swindle having to do with his invention? Did Barry Knight come here trying to prevent it? You see, if all these suppositions are true, we've about reached the point where Barry cannot hope to cover up for his father any longer. While it's true that Barry could hardly be blamed for things his father did while Barry was a boy, now that he is grown up, the matter is drastically different. Suppose his father were caught at some big swindle and was exposed. Think how that would reflect on Barry's reputation. All sorts of insinuations could be made, that he had neglected his father, that he was working with his father, that he knew about it and was covering up for his father, that he was profiting from his father's crimes. A gossip columnist like Marv Lister could have a Roman holiday on fare like that, particularly if it were made worth his while, and we can bet that Uglancie would see to that. Maybe that was the sort of thing Barry Knight was afraid of all the time."

"Where do you think Desmond is now, Ron?"

"Well, there's still a chance that he's one of the three guests at the lodge. But if not it's more likely that he's holed up in a cabin somewhere near here. Since you've already explored the cabins to the south and east, I would say the chances are that it's to the north, perhaps in Lonely Valley. And since our friend Mr. Bogus has been taking a number of bird walks in that direction—though I'm convinced he knows no more about birds than I do and not half as much as Professor Villinger—all the evidence points to him as the probable victim."

"What do you think the Uglancie crowd is going to do now, Ron?"

"That's a good question, and I wish I had an answer. One handicap we're laboring under is that we don't know how much they know. That they know something is certain, or they wouldn't be here. But that they don't know everything is equally certain, or Marv Lister would be home writing his column. I suspect they don't intend to sit around here idly for an indefinite period of time. On the other hand, they may believe that *we* aren't going to be sitting around idly very long either, and they're waiting for us to make the first move."

"Then what do we do, try to outsit them?"

"Hm, no, I don't much care for the idea. It's not quite in my nature, and I do have a newspaper job I'm supposed to be holding down. Besides, I always feel it's a good idea to seize the initiative yourself when you can. It keeps the opposition off balance, wondering what you're going to do, and they have to plan their moves according to yours. Another angle to it is that we can't be sure what our own teammate, Barry Knight, is going to do next, either. I wonder if this isn't the time to play our trump card."

"You mean something to do with Mr. Knight?"

"Yes. I think it's important that I make a supreme effort to get in touch with Barry Knight just as soon as I can, and if I'm going to get the opportunity, we'll have to find some way to draw off Mr. Knight, Lister, and Grossen. They still aren't sure we're on to Mr. Knight, so I wonder if we can't use him to draw them off on a false trail. Let's look at that map of the cabins you made up."

Ted produced the paper, and Ronald studied it closely. "I think to the south would be the best direction to try to draw them off, and a cabin about three miles or so away ought to be about the right distance. How many of these cabins would be suitable to stay in overnight?"

"Me and how many others?"

"All four of you, I'm hoping."

"I noticed one cabin, this one here." He indicated with his finger. "It was pretty big, and in good condition."

"Any firewood?"

"Oh, yes, a big stack of it around back. I think they like to keep these cabins stocked up in case any of the vacationers should get lost or injured or something like that. There's an unwritten law that if you use up firewood you're supposed to replace it for the next fellow."

"That ought to keep you busy. But, Ted, I'm not sure. I'm a little hesitant about this whole idea. Lister and Grossen may turn a little ugly when they learn what's happened. I don't think they'd try any rough stuff, but if you don't think you want to chance it, then I'm surely not going to tell you you should."

"Why not?" said Ted blithely. "What've I got to lose except my life, my honor, and about fifteen bucks in cold cash?"

"You're positive about it?" said Ronald.

"Of course. After all, I know I've got a brother I can depend on to make sure I get a good obit."

"Well, O.K., Ted." Ronald relaxed a little. "I'd rather be on your end of the deal, but I don't see any way of managing it. Will you go on skis?"

"I don't care much about skiing after dark. But I'd kind of like to try my hand at some of those big snowshoes Hank has hanging on the cloakroom wall."

"That sounds like a better idea. And I think you'd better pack up a knapsack. You'll need some food and a blanket, and you'd better arrange some sort of lamp in case there's nothing there. I imagine you can get everything you need from Mrs. Hudson. But here's how I want you to go about it, Ted. I want you to get your stuff together in the most secretive way you can manage. I don't care if Lister finds out—in fact I hope he does—but I want you to be very careful that you don't give him any indication that you *want* him to find out. That's why I say go ahead as though you *didn't* want him to find out."

Then Ronald unfolded the rest of his plan. Just inside the back door was a long room called the cloakroom. The guests rarely went there, since they usually used the front door and kept their clothing in their own rooms. However, special outdoor coats and boots were kept there, along with skis, snow-shoes, and other articles. The cloakroom was divided into several compartments, which fitted in with Ronald's plan.

He and Ted would carry their outdoor clothes down to the cloakroom, making quite sure Mr. Knight saw them in the process. Ronald felt certain that within a few minutes Mr. Knight would follow them out. Meanwhile he and Ted would be talking in one of the compartments so that Mr. Knight would be sure to overhear. They rehearsed their conversation a couple of times, then took their coats downstairs and went out to the cloakroom. Shortly afterward they heard its door opening quietly, and were confident their plan was succeeding.

"This is the way we'll work it," said Ronald in a low, urgent voice to Ted. "I want you to leave directly after supper. You've got your coat out here, so you should be able to get off without attracting any attention. Meanwhile, I'll leave to go down to the village where I'll pick up the brief case. I won't return here, but will go directly to the cabin from there. Whosit and his friend will also be leaving separately, in order not to arouse attention, and we'll all meet at the cabin around eight thirty. Have you got all that?"

"I've got it," Ted affirmed.

"I can't afford any slip-up now. You're sure you know the cabin I mean?"

"Yes, I'm sure. I go directly south from here, till the trail branches off at that little clump of fir trees. I take the eastward trail from there that winds through those low hills. About half a mile in there's an old, abandoned cabin with the door hanging on a hinge, but that's not the one I want. From there on the trail leads uphill, and it's on a little round knoll that I'll find the cabin I want."

"That's it, Ted. I imagine we'll all be able to get there without too much trouble, before Lister and Grossen suspect anything at all."

"You're sure they don't suspect already, Ron?"

"I don't see how they can. They don't even know that Whosit's friend is around here, and he's the important one in the deal. I think we can close it out and get away from here before they even know what's happened. We won't come back here at all, but will send for our things."

"What about afterward, though, Ron? What will they do then?"

"What can they do? With the deal closed, they'll never be able to prove that Barry had anything to do with it, and we'll be in for our fifteen-per-cent cut. Barry's got a story all ready about being laid up in a hospital for this past week, with some hospital receipts to prove it."

They heard the door closing very quietly again, and looked out cautiously. The cloakroom was empty once more, and they smiled at each other in triumph.

"The only trouble," said Ted with a smirk, "is that I wish I knew what we were talking about. Say, Ron, suppose that isn't Barry Knight in the northeast room, what are you going to do then?"

"Then I'm going to hunt up the nearest cave and become a hermit. I can just imagine a telegram from Burnett telling me that Barry *has* been in the hospital for the past week, and what the devil am I doing out here anyway?"

The supper bell had rung while they were talking, and they went in to eat. The meal was a repetition of their noontime dinner, except that conversation was a little more subdued. Lister wasn't as obtrusive as usual, nor was Mr. Bogus, while even Professor Villinger seemed to have some important matters to meditate upon. Yet underneath the appearance of calm was a feeling of mounting tension sizzling through the room. The only person who seemed unaware of it was Mr. Lane-Payne, who continued to prattle away quite happily.

As they left the dining room, Mr. Bogus made a point of coming over and shaking hands with Ronald and Ted.

"I guess this is good-by, gentlemen. The birds here will have to get along without me for another season. I'll be going to bed early to make an early start in the morning, so I may not see you again, and I want to thank everybody here who helped make my visit so pleasant."

"The bus doesn't leave till afternoon, does it?" Ronald inquired.

"No, but I understand there are private cars for hire available in the village, so that seems quicker than waiting around. Oh, there's the professor. I want to say good-by to him, too, even though he did create some serious doubts in my mind about that scarlet tanager. But not those new fellows—they don't appeal very much to me. Oh, professor, just a moment," and he hurried off.

Ronald wasn't quite satisfied. If Mr. Bogus was leaving, that meant the deal he was working on was finished. Had he completed it, or had it fallen through? Which way was it? It seemed rather silly to worry about it, though, for Mr. Bogus gave the impression of being a man well able to take care of himself.

Ted went through with his part of the arrangement, slipping out the back door with his knapsack and snowshoes. Ronald left more openly, saying he was going for a stroll down to the village. But he did not go very far in that direction before he circled around to the rear of the lodge where he took up his station behind a group of trees. There he was able to watch what was going on at the lodge without fear of being observed.

Not long after Ted had left, Mr. Knight also left, heading in the same direction. Then there was a longer interval, before Marv Lister and Marty Grossen departed, taking the same southern trail. So far everything was going along smoothly. Ronald only hoped that Ted would be all right, but he had a great deal of confidence in his brother's clear-headedness.

Ronald continued to wait. Knowing how far away the cabin was he knew he had at least two or three hours to himself. It wasn't his intention to approach the northeast room directly unless he found time running out and felt that he must. Instead, he decided that Barry Knight would probably be leaving his room by the outside stairway, as he had done the previous day. Therefore, Ronald took up his vigil. The wind was cold, and his legs grew a little stiff from standing, but the light was still on in the northeast room, and that gave him confidence.

At last it was switched off, and Ronald stiffened to attention. A man came out and started down the stairs, but Ronald was not sure who it was. As the man passed the foot of the stairs, the light from a downstairs window caught him briefly, and Ronald recognized Barry Knight's loud hunting jacket. He breathed a deep sigh of relief.

He stepped forward to intercept the young reporter he had come so far to find. "Well, Knight," he announced, "it took me quite a while, but I finally made it."

"That you, Wilford? I might have known I couldn't throw you off my trail. I hope I didn't give you too much trouble?"

"It wasn't so bad, although the name threw me for a while. You're Lawrence Desmond, aren't you?"

"That's right."

"And your father is Walter Desmond, the man who went to prison for a gas-station robbery?"

"You're wrong about that, Wilford," said Knight earnestly. "My father went to prison all right, but he didn't steal the money. I know that he couldn't have taken it, because I was there at the time."

CHAPTER 17

Hostile Faces

The snowshoes felt strange and cumbersome on Ted's feet, but it didn't take him long to get the hang of them, and by keeping his feet spread far enough apart he managed pretty well. The snow had drifted high in some places, but the snowshoes buoyed him up so well that he probably made much better progress than he would have without them.

Reaching the small clump of trees to the south, he swung around to the eastward. Here the going became more treacherous, and he had to watch himself. It was uphill as well, and the trail was difficult to hold. He was secretly pleased at whatever difficulties he met, because he knew that the persons he had every reason to believe would soon be following him would experience equal or greater difficulties. This meant Ronald would have ample time to make his arrangements with Barry Knight.

The first cabin was quickly found and passed, and he worked his way upward along the winding trail. He had been there earlier in the day, but things looked strangely different at night. There was no moon, but he had never seen the stars shining so brilliantly. Orion was one of the prominent constellations in the sky, a friendly, familiar sight. There were not a great many trees, but those there were looked bleak and black against the night sky. It would have been nearly impossible to find his way had it not been for the white snow, which caught the little light there was and reflected it upward. Presently he took out his flashlight as well, which helped him see the immediate path ahead, although the limited length of its beam did not help much to orient him with his surroundings.

He found himself listening as he walked, but heard nothing except the steady crunch of his own shoes on the snow. It wasn't exactly a pleasant sensation to realize that somewhere on the trail behind him were three men—at least he hoped there were. These three men in no sense of the word could be called friends, nor was he certain to just what lengths they might go to express their enmity. While they probably held no personal animosity toward him, he was becoming increasingly aware that big things were at stake in whatever game was being played. A state-wide slot-machine racket, a possible million-dollar invention, and the reputation of a well-known newspaperman were no mere trifles.

The prominent knoll presently came into sight, and he climbed up to the cabin above. His long hike had exhilarated him, and he felt the warm glow of his cheeks and the steady thumping of his pulse as he stooped to remove the snowshoes, then pushed open the door of the cabin.

There was a kerosene lamp inside, so he didn't need to use the shorter-lived electric lamp he had brought with him. He lit the wick and carefully replaced the chimney. Within the cabin were a table with two attached benches, a fireplace, a cupboard, and something that only in the most general sense could be described as a bed. It was a wooden frame with wires strung across, possibly intended to hold some soft boughs before it was occupied, but Ted felt it would be just as wise to sleep on the floor. Anyway, if Mr. Knight, Lister, and Grossen all arrived, there probably wouldn't be much sleep for any of them. Ted would have much preferred to leave them all there while he made the run back to the lodge, even in the middle of the night, but those weren't Ronald's orders. Ronald had told him to hold them there as long as he could, which probably meant he must stay all night.

He would have to make a fire, and since there was no back door, he went from the front of the cabin to the woodpile in the back. He made several trips, until he had sufficient wood to last at least for a few hours. Building a fire in the fireplace, he added wood chips and an old newspaper he found, and put a match to it. The fire caught almost at once, the chimney drew well, and soon a big blaze was crackling, sending its warmth circulating through the room. Ted took off his coat and sat down on the floor near the fire until the heat drove him back to the table. Surely the others would be along soon if they were coming, and he awaited them with mixed feeling—hopeful that their plan was successful, but with some apprehension about what he could say or do.

He heard a noise outside and swung his eyes to the door. It opened slowly, and he saw that it was not the men he had expected, or at least not all of them. Mr. Knight alone came into the room. Had their plan been a failure then? Had the opposition split their forces, sending Mr. Knight along here while the others kept an eye on Ronald?

"Hello, Ted," said Mr. Knight, beginning to open his coat. "That's a pretty good fire you've got there. I'll be glad to stand up against it for a while. Old bones take longer to warm up than young ones like yours."

"What do you want here?" said Ted suspiciously, and there was no friendliness in his tone. He felt a little angry that Ronald had been apparently outwitted, and wondered what kind of bluff Mr. Knight would put up.

"Now, Ted, is that the way to talk to me, after we've been friends for a few days and come so far together? I don't mind telling you what I want. I had a hunch from the way you took your coat downstairs just before supper that you were going to sneak out somewhere, and the thought came to me that maybe you had some line on where my son was and weren't telling me. So I thought I'd just better tag along, and I must say you led me quite a chase. Is Barry coming here tonight, Ted? Is that why you're here? If you only knew how anxious I am to see my son after so many years, I'm sure you wouldn't refuse to tell me."

So that was the line he was going to take. He was still pretending to be Barry Knight's father, although Ted knew by now that there wasn't a chance in the world of its being so. Didn't Mr. Knight know that his bluff had been called by this time? Surely he would know that the first time Ronald talked to Barry Knight, Barry would tell him so. It was on the tip of Ted's tongue to tell Mr. Knight that his little game was known, but wisely Ted checked himself. He couldn't be sure yet that it really was Barry Knight in the northeast room. Even if it was, maybe Mr. Knight didn't know about it, and so it was better to keep him guessing.

"I'm afraid I don't know for sure where Barry Knight is," Ted replied, "but at least I'm pretty certain he isn't coming here tonight."

"Then who is coming, Ted? Surely you wouldn't have come all the way up here just to be by yourself. Are you expecting someone else?"

Ted said truthfully, "It's beginning to look as if those I was expecting aren't going to show up."

Mr. Knight had little more to say. Ted wasn't going to tell him, and he couldn't sound too pressing without exposing himself. So he eased over to the fire and rubbed his hands.

"Something about a good, friendly fire," he remarked. "It gives off a kind of warmth that you never get from a stove or a radiator. Maybe it's the color of the flames that makes it seem so cheerful. Sure you got enough wood, Ted? This won't last the night."

"Maybe it won't have to last the night," said Ted bluntly.

"You ain't going back to the lodge tonight, are you? I don't much hanker for that long walk again. Fact is, I'm not sure I could find my way alone in the dark. I only made it up here by following your trail."

"You can stay or leave as you please," Ted told him. He decided to carry along with Mr. Knight's bluff for a while. "Ron has told me how you neglected Barry when he was a little boy. I don't think I could feel much friendship toward a man like that."

"Ah, well," said Mr. Knight humbly, "you've got to forgive an old man for mistakes he made a long time ago."

What ought he to do? Ted wondered. Just staying at the cabin alone with Mr. Knight wasn't going to do Ronald any good, was it? Maybe his best course was to hurry back to the lodge and warn Ronald. But what good would it do after all? It was a long hike back to the lodge, and surely Ronald must have been aware by this time of the miscarriage of their plans. Probably it was better to play the game out to the end along the lines Ronald had indicated.

And fifteen minutes later Ted was glad he had made the decision he did. There was a little commotion outside, and once more the door opened. Marv Lister, followed closely by Marty Grossen, came into the room. They pulled off their gloves and blew on their fingers. Outside the wind was picking up a little, and they could hear its low whistle.

Mr. Knight expressed surprise at seeing the newcomers, but Lister immediately cut him off. "You can forget it. You aren't fooling anybody, and I'm not sure you ever did. Wilford must surely have talked to Barry Knight by now, and he knows you're not Knight's father. We don't need you anymore. We'll pay you off, and you can go your own way."

Turning upon Mr. Knight, Ted said, "Was that all you were in this for—as just a way to pick up a little money? Didn't you care what happened to Barry Knight?"

"That wasn't it at all, Ted. Let me explain—"

"I don't think it's necessary for you to explain anything," said Ted abruptly.

"Well, what's going on here, Ted?" said Lister, bustling about. "What are you up here for?"

"I might ask the same thing of you," Ted returned sharply.

"You know why I'm up here. I'm here because I figured something was going on. A conference, isn't it? Well, where is everybody?"

"I'm sure I don't have any idea who 'everybody' means."

"You know who I mean—your brother, Barry Knight, Desmond, and Mr. Bogus. They were all getting together tonight on a deal, weren't they? This gent who calls himself Mr. Bogus wasn't fooling anybody with his line about going to bed early so he could get an early start tomorrow. I know who he is, and I'm pretty sure your brother does, too—and I know for certain he didn't come up here just to listen to the pretty birds."

"I wouldn't know anything about that," Ted answered. "I don't know who Mr. Bogus is, and whatever his plans are, he sure didn't tell them to me."

Grossen gave Lister a nudge of his elbow, and said hoarsely, "This don't look like a conference to me. I wonder if we didn't come to the wrong place."

"You could be right, Grossen, and if you are it's the second time you've been right this year. You were right about Mr. Bogus going up to meet Desmond in Lonely Valley." He remarked in an aside to the others, "It isn't often he's right twice in the same year."

"He wasn't right when he searched my suitcase on the train," Ted broke in.

"A small thing, Ted. He was in Forestdale at the time, checking out the possibility that Barry Knight was hiding at your home. He was then ordered to follow you to Union City, but searching your suitcase was his own idea, and not a very good one. He didn't find anything, so there's no reason to get sore. In fact, I don't see any reason at all why we shouldn't be friends even though your brother works for a different paper. There's usually a pretty good fellowship among members of the press, and they don't mind giving each other little tips from time to time. I've just got a few little questions to ask you, and I don't think you'll mind telling me as one newspaperman to another. Is there a conference going on up in Lonely Valley tonight? Is that where everybody is, while your brother very cleverly sent you out to lead the opposition astray?"

"I don't know anything about it," Ted replied, "and if I did, I surely wouldn't tell you."

"Oh, we haven't got time to fool around with him," said Grossen impatiently. "Mr. Big ain't gonna like it when he finds out we been wastin' our time one place when we should have been someplace else. I can get it out of him in a couple of minutes."

Lister shrugged. "I like to do things a little more subtly than that, but if you must..."

Grossen suddenly stepped behind Ted and bent his arm up behind his back. Stinging pains shot up to Ted's shoulder, and he winced in spite of himself. He looked about. Lister had turned away indifferently. The unconcealed hatred in Grossen's face was clearly evident. Even Mr. Knight evidently wasn't going to interfere.

"Where's the conference tonight?" said Grossen menacingly, bringing Ted's arm up sharply once more.

"I don't know!" Ted cried.

"We think you do. Ask him some more questions, Lister. He's gonna think up some answers pretty soon or else..."

"Who is this man named Desmond?" said Lister carelessly. "I haven't been able to get much of a line on him yet. Is he a relative of Knight's or is theirs just a business relationship?"

Ted gritted his teeth but said nothing, and once more his arm was forced upward. The pain went through him like a knife. Hold on, don't let them intimidate you, he told himself. They don't dare really hurt me, they're not so all-powerful that they can get away with anything. This is as much as they dare do to me, and if I can take this much, then they're licked.

"No answer to that, Ted?" said Lister smoothly. "Then let's try once more. I wouldn't want Grossen to get really rough, but sometimes I have difficulty controlling him. Another thing I'd like to know is Barry Knight's real name. Do you know anything about that?"

As Ted hesitated, his arm went upward once more, this time harder, longer, and steadier, with his wrist turned back as well. He tried to lean forward to break the grip, but Grossen's other arm was firmly about him. I've had a broken ankle this past year, and I can take a broken arm if I have to, he reminded himself. More than the pain, the hot blood of frustration was rushing to his cheeks, a sense of futility and helplessness because he knew it was useless to fight back. Up until now he had considered feeding them little dabs of useless information, but now he was mad. He controlled himself with difficulty, knowing that anger would only add to his plight, that if he got to talking he might give something away that would help them.

"You can save all your trouble," he said stoutly, "because I'm not going to tell you anything at all!"

Again his arm went up, bring sharper pains that made him think that this time his arm really would break. But Mr. Knight had moved away from the fireplace and out to the center of the scene.

"Well, now," he offered mildly, "it seems to me that maybe we are exceeding our instructions just a little."

"That's right, let him go," Lister ordered. "I can't afford to get mixed up in something like this, and I forgot we had a witness. Besides, that's not the proper way to deal with a boy like Ted. Let me talk to him."

Reluctantly Grossen released his grasp. The soreness gradually disappeared from Ted's arm, but he was far from soothed.

"Ted, you want to be a newspaperman, don't you?"

"This is your build-up," said Ted bitingly. "You can carry on without answers from me."

"I know you're interested in newspaper work. Editor of your school paper, high-school correspondent for the town paper, a brother on a bigcity paper. I was once a sincere, idealistic boy very much like you, so I think I can understand you. You've been bit by the bug early, just the way I was. Now as an incipient newspaperman, you believe in freedom of the press, I'm sure."

At least this was one response Ted could make without compromising himself. "Yes, I do."

"All right, then, that's it." He waved his arm as though there was no further room for argument. "If you believe in freedom of the press, you believe in the right of a newspaper reporter to get a story if he can. And all I want is a story."

"I don't care much for your kind of story," said Ted firmly. "You haven't any right to intrude into a person's private life unless there is some public purpose to be served."

"You mean if a person commits a crime the paper shouldn't tell about it?"

"That's different. Enforcement of the law is a matter of public concern. That's not the same as the kind of gossip you peddle."

"I take it you don't approve of my work. Well, let me tell you something, Ted. If you ever rise as high as I have in the newspaper world, you'll have reason to be satisfied, and glad, and proud. Over a hundred papers carry my column—"

"But the *Twilight Star* isn't one of them," Ted reminded him.

"I see. The *Star* is a special paragon of virtue, just because your brother works there. Let me tell you that the *Star* is a paper just like the others, and their reporters grub for stories just the way other reporters do. Whether or not you approve of my delving into the lives of other people, you must agree that a newspaper reporter's life is a special case. Barry Knight never hesitated to examine someone else's life for the sake of a story. A person in that position ought to be willing to hold up his own life for examination, and I'm beginning to get the feeling that Barry Knight has a good deal to hide. When the public is relying upon his integrity, I've got a right to make sure the public isn't being fooled, haven't I? That's all I'm trying to do."

"You can try," Ted asserted, "but you aren't going to get any help from me."

"I still don't think you quite understand the situation, Ted. Now you're a friend of Barry Knight's, or at least your brother is, and I'm sure you'd like to help him if you could. I don't have anything against Knight—the last thing in the world I want is to do anything to hurt him. Unfortunately he is in a position where he can hurt some other people I know. Why should anybody get hurt at all, when we can make a little deal?"

So that was what they really wanted, Ted thought—not to expose Barry Knight, but to get something on him and then make a trade. They would trade what they knew about Knight for what Knight knew about Uglancie. But even if Knight were willing to agree to a proposition like this, it would mean that he would have a club hanging over his head for the rest of his career.

"I've never met Barry Knight," said Ted firmly, "but from the things I've heard about him, I think you'd be wasting your breath."

An impasse seemed to have developed. Ted wondered what they would do next. Would they turn him over to Grossen again? He had already made up his mind that he wasn't going to let Grossen touch him again without a struggle. If they wanted a brawl, they were going to get it.

A booming sound came to their ears, followed by a distant rumble. Thunder in the winter? Ted wondered. It sometimes happened, but he hadn't seen any lightning. Or was it something else?...

"What was that?" he demanded.

"Oh, that?" said Lister, as though it didn't matter. "Avalanche, I guess. The professor was due to blow up the hill at Lonely Valley tonight. That's why I was so sure the conference wouldn't be held there tonight. Maybe I was wrong, but if I was, maybe your brother was just as wrong."

CHAPTER 18

Rendezvous at Lonely Valley

The two men stared at each other in the glow from the window reflected upon the snow. Ronald was the younger by several years, the new, inexperienced recruit who had just begun to feel his way into a newspaper career, while Barry Knight was the established reporter who had already made his mark and was still moving upward. Ronald had looked up to Knight as an ideal, and had tried to pattern his work after the older man's.

"You're certain he's innocent?" Ronald asked skeptically.

"I'm positive. There was just no way he could possibly have taken the money. I'll tell you about it on our way up. I suppose you've already guessed that my father's been staying up at Lonely Valley. Bill was keeping him supplied until I came here, but now I've been taking care of it." He shifted the bundle he was carrying to the other arm. "Want to come along?"

"If I may. Think we're all right in just our overshoes?"

"Oh, yes, it isn't too bad walking. I've done it before." They started out toward the head of the northern valley. In the darkness Ronald could easily have lost his way, but Knight went ahead with assurance.

"You mentioned someone named Bill," Ronald reminded him. "I haven't met anyone here yet by that name."

"I meant Bill Hudson, of course. That's his real name, William Hudson, but the nickname Hank fits in better with the name of the lodge. My father and I knew Hudson and his wife back in the old days at Imperial, before they left to start their lodge up here. So when my father needed a rather quiet, isolated place where he could conduct a business arrangement, he immediately came here."

"And you followed him," Ronald added. "I think it was that hunting jacket of yours that finally gave it away to me. I figured when you'd taken your jacket along you must have had someplace like this in mind."

"Well, you certainly came to the right place, Wilford, but for the wrong reason. When I left town I had no idea where I was likely to end up beyond Union City. I knew vaguely that Hudson and his wife had left Imperial years before to start some sort of lodge, but I had no idea where, and no particular reason to believe my father had gone to them. It was the poster in the lobby of the hotel at Union City that put me on the track. I immediately realized that Hank Hudson must be the old Bill Hudson who was a friend of my father's, and that that must be where he had gone, so I never stopped to register at the hotel at all."

"So then I was wrong about one more thing," said Ronald, more than a little vexed with himself. "I've made so many blunders on this case that it isn't funny."

"I wouldn't call it a blunder, Wilford. Your logic was a little faulty, but your intuition was sound. It was the same sort of intuition that led me to take my hunting jacket along in the first place when I didn't know where I was going—just the feeling that I was likely to end up in some such place as this. Intuition is more subtle than logic only because it's based on smaller things that we can't quite put our finger on, but are there just the same. You've explained how you got from Union City to Half Moon Lodge, but you haven't yet explained how you got as far as Union City."

"Dixie Orlando tipped me off," Ronald admitted.

"He did? You were pretty smart to catch on to Orlando, and even then it must have taken some persuasion. He's a fairly closemouthed type."

"I managed to convince him that you might be in some sort of danger, and even then he wouldn't tell me until I convinced him that I already knew something about Walter Desmond. He's quite a character, isn't he?"

"Oh, yes, a character all right, but loyal as a dog, and he's been plenty useful to me on a number of occasions. I'll have to take you down to Short Vincent sometime and have you meet some of these characters—if I ever go back."

"Then you may not go back?" asked Ronald, narrowing his eyes.

"I don't know, Wilford," Knight responded, and all the weariness, frustration, and despair that had led him to Half Moon Lodge showed in his voice. "I can't tell yet how things are going to turn out. I'll do whatever I have to do."

He stopped speaking, and although Ronald was filled with questions he wanted to ask, he felt it was best to let Knight tell it in his own way and in his own good time. But Knight made no attempt to go on, and they trudged in silence for several minutes.

"You knew about Marv Lister and Marty Grossen being here, didn't you?" asked Ronald at last.

"Oh, yes, Bill's been keeping me posted on everything."

"That's a funny thing," said Ronald, feeling it might put Knight more at ease if he adopted a lighter attitude. "I can't get used to that name Bill. My brother was just pointing out to me how many persons here are going around under assumed names. One of the reasons I felt I couldn't talk things over with Hank—or Bill—was because I didn't know what name you were using, and I didn't want to give too much away."

"Bill doesn't know anything about Barry Knight—I doubt if he's so much as heard the name before. He remembered me as Larry Desmond from the Imperial days."

"How's that name again?" said Ronald, screwing up his face, for ever since that call from Carole he had been careful to use the more common pronunciation of Desmond, but Knight had just pronounced it as though it were French.

"It's a French name," Barry told him, "and my family's always clung to the French pronunciation, even though most people who didn't know us very well used the other way."

"Well," said Ronald, brightening, "maybe I won't come out of this affair so badly after all, although I gave your secretary a bad time for a while."

"Carole? This was a tough break on her. I know she felt she had a rather intimate knowledge of my affairs, and this must have seemed like a dirty deal to her. Does she resent it very much?"

"I don't think Carole is the kind of person who could hold a grudge even if she wanted to," said Ronald with emphasis, and Knight laughed in spite of himself.

"You haven't told me yet how you know your father was innocent," Ronald reminded him. "Feel like talking about it?"

"Oh, I don't mind. I think I've been quiet altogether too long. There seems to have been a conspiracy to keep me quiet, but that's over now. I'll tell you just what my father did that night, Wilford."

Pausing as though to collect his thoughts, he went on in a moment, "As you know my father worked at the gas station. He put in long hours, which included a good deal of overtime, so that I got to hanging around the station, too, when I didn't have anything else to do. On the night of the robbery there was a basketball game at school, which kept me rather late. On the way home I stopped off at the station, as I often did, to wait for my father. It was just about time to close up, and I saw my father go over to the cash register. He took out the money and counted it, to compare it with the total on the cash register. It came out all right, so he put it back. Remember that, Wilford, *I saw him put it back.*

"About that time a friend of his came past. I would have gone out to service the car, as I occasionally did. There was a drizzle coming down, and I figured my father'd been out in it enough. However, he said his friend wanted to talk over something or other, and there wasn't any use in both of us getting wet. So I waited in the station while he went out and talked. It turned out that this friend of his didn't really want anything except to talk.

"After about ten minutes the friend drove off and my father came back into the station. Since his friend hadn't bought anything, there was no need for my father to go over to the cash register again. As a matter of fact, he didn't go near the cash register—I'm positive of that. We were late already and wet and a little cold and anxious to get home. So my father set the alarm, turned out the light, locked up, and we went on home."

"Could he have come back later during the night?" Ronald queried closely.

"Impossible. I'm certain that the burglar alarm was already set. Besides, I was feeling a little restless that night after all the excitement of the basketball game—I scored the tying point in the last few seconds of play, but we lost in overtime—and I'm certain if my father got up and went out I would have heard him."

"Then how do you figure the robbery?" Ronald asked him.

"Why do I have to figure it?" Barry cried out bitterly. "My father was innocent and I know it. Isn't that enough?"

"You'd think it ought to be," said Ronald, more disturbed than his voice showed, "but very often it isn't. How did it happen you weren't called to testify at the trial?"

"Because our lawyer wouldn't put me on the stand," said Barry, still bitter at the recollection. "He gave me a long spiel about how he felt it would hurt my father's chances rather than help him. I don't know just what it was all about. I think he was trying to create some doubt in the jurors' minds that the burglar alarm really had been set at the time my father left the station. What could I say? I knew the alarm had been set. I remembered it distinctly. I'm not pretending to be too good, Wilford. I would have lied on the witness stand if I thought it would have done my father any good. But our lawyer was a completely honest man, even though I have some doubts about his competence. He would never consent to having me go on the witness stand and lie. He didn't state it to me in those terms. He said if I went on the stand and lied, a smart lawyer would be able to get me all twisted up under cross-examination, and that would wreck our case. Another point was that if I went on the stand, he felt my father would have to support my testimony, and for some reason he felt it was better for my father not to testify. I don't know exactly what was going on in his mind. I think he honestly thought my father was mistaken about setting that burglar alarm when he left, even though my father swore that he did, and he didn't want him to say that under cross-examination, just as he didn't want me to say it.

"Another point was that he didn't want the facts about my father's past conviction to be introduced into the trial. I think there's some rule of law or other that the prosecution can't introduce testimony about past convictions, but if my father went on the stand and testified about his past life, then the prosecution under cross-examination might be able to bring this point out. The particular rule of law involved wasn't clear to me then, and isn't clear to me now.

"Anyway, for reasons that seemed all right to me at the time, I was kept off the witness stand. As a matter of fact, I wasn't even present at the trial. My father said he didn't want me to miss school, but I imagine his more real concern was that he wanted to spare me the ordeal of the trial.

"I believe our lawyer really thought my father was innocent. He felt the best defense would be merely to introduce some character witnesses for my father, along with a little expert testimony on locks and things. I saw my father and the lawyer every day after court was adjourned. They acted cheerful and led me to believe things were going very well. It was only when I read about the trial afterward that I learned how strong the prosecution case was, and how feeble the defense was. We merely had a few witnesses like Doctor Milton, who said they had always thought my father was a good man, and then there was a locksmith who said, well, maybe this could have happened, or maybe that could have happened. His testimony wavered so that it wouldn't have convinced anybody. And my father's story of what happened that night was never presented to the jury at all, which must have seemed suspicious to them. But at the time I was feeling rather optimistic. I knew my father was innocent, and I simply couldn't believe that an innocent man would be convicted.

"When I heard the news of the verdict I was completely stunned. One to ten years on a false charge! I felt now that a serious mistake had been made in not putting me on the stand. I pleaded with the lawyer to do something, try for a new trial, take my deposition, anything—but he soothed me over. He explained to me that one to ten years really meant my father could apply for a parole in about nine months. Even a new trial, if he could gain it, might produce the same result, and meanwhile the time my father was serving wouldn't count toward his sentence. My father didn't want to appeal, but felt that the best thing would be to begin serving his sentence at once.

"Then I talked to my father. He spoke to me cheerfully, as though he didn't really mind the sentence, and assured me that it wouldn't seem so long. He spoke to me of some of his hopes for me, assured me there was nothing I could do or say that would change the verdict, and said he wanted me to go on and work hard and finish school. Perhaps he would be seeing me not long after that, but in case he didn't, I was to try to build the best sort of life that I could for myself. He didn't tell me he was innocent—we both knew that he was and it wasn't necessary to say it—and his final words were to give me his fondest blessing. When they took him away, I sat down and cried like a baby. Even then I had hopes of seeing him in nine months. I didn't know it would stretch out to six years.

"Well, I went on, of course. Things weren't the same as they had been before. I was inclined to be unusually sensitive, and this trial hadn't helped me any, so I imagined everybody was pointing the finger of scorn at me. I dropped off the basketball team, dropped out of pretty nearly everything. About all I did was go to school and come home and study, so that I managed to finish with high marks, as my father had hoped for me.

"Our home was closed down, and I boarded with a family in the village. We weren't well to do, but my father had some savings, and along with what I could earn at odd jobs it was enough to see me through school. You can understand how it hurt to realize the money I was living on could have been used to appeal my father's case and might have freed him. Don, down at the service station, was very kind to me and offered to let me work there, but that was one job I wouldn't take. I felt that his testimony was principally responsible for sending my father to prison, and that he could have saved him if he had tried.

"I graduated from high school the following June. I imagine you can understand by now why I was anxious to get away from Imperial, and after getting the minister to write me a letter of recommendation, I left the village and came on to the city. I still felt a sense of guilt and shame over the trial so I thought I ought to change my name, and I'm afraid I committed an act of forgery on the minister's letter. Anyway, I was hired by the newspaper, which didn't check my reference just as I had hoped, and I guess you can pretty well carry the story on from there."

"Did you keep in touch with your father while he was in prison?" Ronald inquired of him.

"No, Wilford, I didn't—not directly, though I kept informed of his circumstances. There had been something between us that would be hard to explain, a kind of respect and esteem we had always felt for each other. Somehow the trial had changed that. I hadn't testified for him, and he had concealed from me the old crime he had committed as a young man, something I never knew about until he was sentenced to prison again. I knew that my father still held as much affection for me as he ever did, but that old feeling of mutual trust had somehow vanished between us. When he got out of prison he made no attempt to look me up, feeling I suppose that his past record might prove a blot on my name. If we were to get together again, I had to find him, and that is just what I did the first chance I could. We met here at Lonely Valley, and I feel that we're now closer together than we ever were before. Between ourselves, the past is wiped clean. Unfortunately, that may not be the end of it. It isn't so easy to clear the slate between ourselves and the rest of the world, and that is the thing that stands between me and my return to the newspaper."

"Your father came up here to negotiate about his invention, didn't he?"

"That's right. I rather thought you'd caught on to that."

"And the man he was negotiating with was Mr. Bogus?"

"You might say that. It's not his real name, of course. Didn't you recognize him? You've met him once before."

"His face did look just a little bit familiar," said Ronald in wonder. "Is he from Detroit?"

"Near Detroit. You've pinned it down close enough."

"Then he was a speaker at that press reception a couple of months back. If he'd happened to speak on birds at the banquet, I would have recognized him this time. Well, I guess I'll just have to chalk that up as another one of my lapses, though it's getting monotonous," he added resignedly.

"Yes, he's the big wind in one of those motor corporations. At the time of the reception I had a private interview with him at which I mentioned my father's invention. He didn't say anything then, nor did I ever hear anything about it afterward. He must have gone directly to my father about it and arranged for a demonstration up here in Lonely Valley."

"Then they have been negotiating?" Ronald asked, remembering that Mr. Bogus was due to leave the lodge. "Did anything come of it?"

"I don't know yet," said Knight tiredly. "That's what I'm anxious to find out."

In spite of their protracted talk, they had been walking fairly rapidly. Ronald had noticed Knight looking at his illuminated wrist watch often, as though trying to time something. They had now reached the mouth of Lonely Valley, and they observed a number of flares up on the hillside, flaming high against the sky, with several black forms flitting about.

"Professor Villinger," Knight explained, "with a couple of assistants from the village. I know he's been worried about this hill for a long time. Something about the decreasing cohesion with the thaw, I've been told."

"Do you think there's any danger in our skirting the bottom of the hill?"

"I wouldn't know. Apparently the professor doesn't think so, or he would have had the bottom of the hill marked out as a danger spot."

"Isn't that a man coming down the hill? Maybe he's going to set up flares down here now."

"Maybe, but let's not wait for him. I'm anxious to get to the cabin. Don't come along if you think it's dangerous."

"Oh, I guess my neck's no more valuable than yours. Let's go."

They made their way around the high drifts of snow lying just below the hills at the entrance to the valley and went on into the valley itself. It was tougher going now, with the hills cutting off much of the light from the sky. There were drifts of snow to be avoided, too, but Knight was apparently well acquainted with the path, and by sticking close behind him Ronald managed to avoid any trouble.

They had proceeded for about half an hour up the valley, and surely must be nearing the cabin, Ronald thought, when there was a sound like a sudden clap of thunder. It was followed after a few seconds' silence by another clap, and there slowly developed the low but mounting rumble of huge blocks of snow breaking off and gathering momentum as they tumbled down into the valley.

CHAPTER 19

A Run through the Night

The distant rumbling came to an end, but the silence was almost as ominous.

"If there was to be dynamiting, why wasn't there some notice?" asked Ted.

"There was," Lister told him. "The bulletin board by the front door had it, but you and your brother were too busy sneaking out the back door. What's the difference? There'll be guards up around the danger area."

"Doesn't an explosion like that sometimes start avalanches on other hills in the area?"

"The professor didn't think it would, and those fellows sometimes know what they're doing."

But the professor could have been wrong, Ted thought, or maybe he was too late. Perhaps this was a real avalanche after all, breaking off before the professor had time to touch off the explosion. Where did this leave Ronald? Had he been in the danger area? There was a good chance he was, for now that Ted knew Mr. Desmond was staying at a cabin up in Lonely Valley, that was probably where Barry Knight had gone the night before. Maybe he had gone again tonight, and Ronald had gone with him.

Ted stood up and stared at the others tensely. "I'm going back to the lodge," he announced, satisfied that there was nothing more he could do here. He reached out for his coat. "Does anybody want to stop me?"

Grossen made a move in his direction, and Ted braced himself to meet him, but Lister dismissed Grossen with a wave of his hand.

"Let him go. I think that Ted all unwittingly has told us exactly what we wanted to know. The conference was in Lonely Valley, not here, but things being what they are, I think I'd just as soon be here as there."

Zipping up his jacket, Ted went out without looking at any of the others. He put on his snowshoes and started down the dark trail. He passed the deserted cabin, and found the clump of trees that served as his landmark. Then he turned to the north. It was a little lighter here now that he was farther away from the low hills, but not enough to help him greatly. Finding it impossible to keep to the trail made by his footprints on the way up, he didn't try, but set his course by dead reckoning. Overhead Orion was still brilliant, but had moved considerably farther to the west.

Time passed as Ted trudged on. Surely Ronald would have been careful, surely he was all right. But the thought that something might have gone wrong lent wings to his steps. The low-lying plain through which he was passing was desolate, swept remorselessly by the wind until the ground was nearly bare in spots. There were few trees, he saw no other persons, no trace of human habitation.

He had forgotten to look at his watch when he left the cabin, so he had no idea how long he had been out. But it was beginning to seem long—too long. The lights of the lodge should have come into sight before this. Maybe he had passed it, maybe the low hill back of the lodge had cut off his vision and he hadn't noticed. Panic urged him to turn around, retrace his steps, take a wide circle in the hopes of picking up the lodge, but he forced himself to be calm.

He tried to work out his situation logically. If he really was past the lodge and was still heading north, he was in trouble. He couldn't be sure of finding shelter, and while he felt that if necessary he could keep on walking all night so he wouldn't freeze, there was still no assurance he would be able to find his way in the morning. This wilderness was tricky. He might actually be very close to home without realizing it. Even a searching party, if one should be dispatched, might not find him in time.

On the other hand if he started circling around wildly and aimlessly, he was likely to get nowhere at all. He would soon be hopelessly confused, and might finally drop in his tracks. If he could find the footprints he or the others had made on their way up he would be all right, but with the freshening wind carrying the snow across the ground in little gusts, there seemed only a remote chance of that.

When you don't know what to do, the best thing is to act as logically as you can, Ted decided. Where had he made a mistake, where had he gone wrong? Chances were that his time sense had failed him, and that he hadn't been en route nearly as long as he thought. He looked at his watch, trying to decide the very minimum of time that he had been on the trail. When he had arrived at this, he thought that surely another half hour would bring him to the lodge, unless he was lost. The best thing to do was to assume he was on the right path and keep going. If he didn't come to the lodge in half an hour, then he could be sure he had passed it, and would have to try to figure out something else.

And twenty minutes later his logic proved its value as the lodge came into sight. He hadn't been lost at all, only afraid that he might be, which is nearly as bad and sometimes produces the very result that is feared.

Stopping only long enough to divest himself of his snow-shoes, he hurried into the lodge and went directly to the desk.

"Where is my brother?" he asked of Hank.

"Your brother? Ted, I'm not sure—"

"Is he up at Lonely Valley?" he demanded. "Is that where the avalanche took place?"

"Yes, Ted, it was at Lonely Valley, but don't call it an avalanche. It was just that professor playing with his toys. I don't think there was any danger of snowslides; he was just anxious to see if he could set one off by an explosion. Since he had the necessary permits, there was nothing I could do to stop him. At the very least he could have posted the area and put off this business for a couple of days until after you newspapermen had gone home. Unfavorable publicity like this could wreck my business."

"You haven't told me where Ron is," Ted reminded him. "Is he all right?"

"Oh, he must be all right. Larry Desmond knew about the dynamiting, and if he went up to Lonely Valley, it was because he wanted it that way. They must be all right, only it will be a couple of days before the power snow sled will be able to get through to them."

"You mean I'll have to wait a couple of days to find out if Ron is safe?"

"Oh, no, it'll be possible to signal to them from the hills in the morning. But you won't be able to reach him. The hills in Lonely Valley are difficult enough in summer, but completely impassable in winter."

"Hank," said Ted anxiously, "is there anything more you can tell me about this business? I'm pretty sure Ronald didn't know about the dynamiting, and had no idea he was going to be cut off from everything for a few days. This puts me on a spot because I don't know what he would have wanted to do next. I've got to make some effort to get in touch with the newspaper, or they'll wonder what's happened."

"Well, Ted," said Hank thoughtfully, "I think I can tell you pretty much all I know. Larry Desmond told me that he didn't particularly want to meet your brother, but that if he did it would be all right. The thing he was most anxious about was keeping away from Lister."

"Do you know what Larry was doing up here?"

"Oh, yes, he was looking for his father. Walter Desmond was an old friend of mine. He came up here, needing some out-of-the-way place to experiment and conduct a delicate negotiation. The lodge wouldn't do, partly because some of his gadgets were pretty noisy, and partly because Mr. Bogus insisted upon complete privacy, even though Walter Desmond didn't feel that he had anything to hide."

"Then did Mr. Bogus go up to Lonely Valley tonight?"

"Nope, he's in bed and sound asleep. I know because I took him up a cup of coffee not half an hour ago."

So when Mr. Bogus said he wanted to get to bed early to make an early start he had been telling the exact truth. Lister had been wrong, Ted recalled. People who are accustomed to lying often find it difficult to believe that other people aren't lying, too.

That seemed to be all Hank knew or was willing to tell, and Ted finally turned away from the desk. The things Hank had told him went far to confirm some of Ronald's theories, but they still didn't explain everything.

While he was sitting in the reception room wondering what he ought to do next, the front door opened and Mr. Knight came in, somewhat breathless. He saw Ted, and greeted him with a friendly casualness.

"Hello, there, Ted."

But Ted was in no mood to feel sociable. His wrist and biceps still hurt him, and he felt that Mr. Knight was just as bad as the others. Well, maybe not quite as bad, but Ted had no inclination to try to choose between various shades of black.

"No hard feelings about what happened up in the cabin?" said Mr. Knight cheerfully. "I've grown quite attached to you and your brother, and I'd like to be friends with you."

"Why try to be friends with us? We don't care much for Uglancie's kind, and you seem to be just like the others."

"Oh, not like them, surely," Mr. Knight objected. "Just because I took a job—"

"That's it. You didn't care what happened to anybody. It was just a job to you."

"That isn't quite fair, Ted. It was a job, but the job was to find Barry Knight. It didn't include twisting the arm of a high-school boy. I'm an old man, Ted, and there wasn't much I could do for you, but I did stop them from doing that, didn't I? And the very fact that they had a witness to their threats is the best insurance you've got that they'll never bother you again."

Yes, he had stopped them in his own quiet way, Ted recalled. Perhaps he did owe a debt to Mr. Knight after all.

"But what about Barry Knight? Didn't you care what happened to him?"

"Yes, Ted, I did. I'd known Barry Knight slightly down on Short Vincent, heard a little more about him, and all of it good. Let's look at the matter from my point of view. I was offered a job that involved a vacation trip, a generous expense account, and a five-hundred-dollar bonus in case we found Barry Knight. Well, we did find him, I've been paid off, and the job's over. Wouldn't you have taken a job like that?"

"No."

"All right, then, let's try looking at it from another point of view. I knew Barry Knight to be a fine, upstanding newspaperman with a good future ahead of him. But talking to Uglancie, I found out that there appeared to be some sort of ghost in Barry's past. Well, what was the best thing to do? Could Barry go on, always dreading that this ghost might pop out and ruin him? Wouldn't it be much better to bring the ghost into view right now, and help to slay it, so that it could never trouble him again? If I've helped Barry Knight to do that, he may someday regard me as the best friend he ever had."

There was a good deal of sense in what he said, Ted thought, and if he had managed to line his pockets with a goodly quantity of green stuff while he was doing it, wasn't that fairly typical of the world?

"Don't judge people too harshly," Mr. Knight went on. "Take Marty Grossen, for instance. I know you don't think much of him, and quite frankly he's nothing but a big ugly bruiser. He was a person of considerable ambition but didn't have very much on the ball. Given this particular dilemma, this was about the most that life had to offer him.

"Lister is another case. It was perfectly true, as he said to you, that he was once a young, sincere, ambitious person. His trouble was that in his drive to the top he accepted help from the wrong kind of people, and after he got there he found he couldn't throw them off. Now he doesn't care anymore. All he cares about is what's in it for him. It may seem wrong to say it, but maybe it would be worse for him if he did care and still couldn't do anything about it. As an embryonic newspaperman, you may be able to draw your own moral from some of these pitfalls that have trapped others. Excuse me for speaking so philosophically, but we often get to talking this way down on Short Vincent."

"What is this Short Vincent, anyway?" asked Ted, puzzled. "I think I've heard Ron mention it to me once or twice, but it didn't seem to make much sense."

"I'll tell you, Ted. I suppose every city or town has its quota of screwballs, but we happen to have an unusual concentration of them all at one spot. Barry Knight once wrote a story about this street, known as Short Vincent. From your newspaper experience you know that newspapermen don't always find their stories—sometimes they create them.

Now I wouldn't go so far as to say that Barry created Short Vincent. I'll put it to you this way: that if his story wasn't entirely true at the time he wrote it, it became true afterward. After his story came out, everybody on Short Vincent began acting just the way he'd pictured them. They liked it, I guess, and picked it up."

"Are you one of those Short Vincent screwballs?" Ted asked.

"I guess, Ted, that you know enough about me to realize I'm one of those people who's always got an angle. Another person you may have heard about is Dixie Orlando, the man who always eats red jelly beans. His angle is his friendship with Barry. Now you know that newspapers try to keep advertising out of their news columns, and you know, too, that the distinction between publicity and advertising is one that is often difficult to draw. The *Twilight Star* is a newspaper that draws a particularly hard line on publicity. It's said that it's harder to get a story in the *Star* than in any other of the papers.

"Now let's assume someone has a special desire to get a certain item of publicity in the *Star*. Now if there's a suggestion of publicity stunt or advertising angle about it, he knows better than to send it directly to the *Star*—their wastebasket is full of such things. Instead he goes to Dixie Orlando. Orlando whispers just a hint of it to Barry Knight. Knight thinks he's just got a hot tip, follows it up, and because he's produced the story himself instead of having it handed to him he thinks it's great, and the story gets published. Newspaper reporters always like to dig up their own stories—or at least, that's the pattern of this particular operation."

"Didn't Knight know what was going on?"

"Of course he did—he's a pretty shrewd fellow. That's why a good many of the fellows have been wishing for some time that the *Star* would send down a less experienced reporter. But very often Knight thought the story was good enough to use just the same. As long as the story appeared, Dixie Orlando was in a position to take credit for it, and to collect his pay-off from the person wanting the publicity in the first place. On the other hand, Knight often paid Orlando for some of his really good tips, so Orlando has a good thing coming from both sides."

"Is that the angle they have down on Short Vincent?" asked Ted.

"That's just one of the angles. On Short Vincent everybody's got his own angle."

Life must often get pretty complicated on Short Vincent, Ted decided. But meanwhile he still had his own worry about Ronald's safety and what was going on up in Lonely Valley. At the moment there seemed nothing to do about it except sit there and sweat it out.

CHAPTER 20

Which Story?

Ronald with Barry Knight stood in tense silence as the rumble grew, until its crescendo sounded like the rolling of a thousand kettledrums. Then came a crash, followed by another and another, with others in such quick succession that one ran into the other and they could not be distinguished. There was one final crash, louder than the others, and then suddenly silence settled over the valley.

"Avalanche!" Ronald exclaimed unnecessarily.

"Not a real avalanche," said Knight, more calmly. "The professor was getting so worried about the hill that he thought he couldn't put it off any longer. Tonight was his time for touching off his explosions. There was a notice posted on the bulletin board at the lodge, but you developed a sudden addiction for the back door, and of course Bill Hudson had let the professor know that he didn't favor that kind of talk at the table. There were other bulletins posted down at the village, and the flares must have been set out just after we passed. Besides, they chose to set the charges off during the night, when nobody would be around."

"At least you could have told me about it," said Ronald resentfully.

"I gave you your chance to go back if you wanted to. Nothing's going to happen except that we'll be marooned up here for a couple of days. That suits my purpose fine, and I think you may find yourself just as well satisfied to be cut off from Lister for a few days."

"What's Ted going to think?"

"Bill Hudson knows the story. He'll explain it to him."

Whether Ronald liked it or not, there was nothing he could do about it. Anyway, he knew he hadn't yet heard the end of the story about Knight and Desmond, and he was anxious to get the remaining details. If only he were sure Ted would be able to deal with Lister—that was his chief worry.

They pushed on to the cabin, which was lighted up and had a spiral of smoke easing lazily out the chimney. After knocking the loose snow off their overshoes, they went inside. The man who came out of the back room to greet them was about fifty, with his hair well streaked with gray and a friendly, welcoming smile on his face.

"Dad, this is a colleague of mine, Ronald Wilford," Knight introduced. "The paper sent him up to find me."

"They must feel you're pretty important, son, to send a man like Mr. Wilford out after you. Make yourself at home, Mr. Wilford. I'll take your coat."

The two young men stepped closer to the fireplace to warm themselves as Mr. Desmond left the room with their coats. When he returned, Knight said:

"Wilford knows something about your invention, Dad. Maybe he'd like you to show it to him."

Mr. Desmond exhibited no reluctance as he picked up the lamp and led the way out the door to a lean-to built flush up against the cabin and fitted out as a workroom. It was cooler here, and the wind whistled through the chinks.

Ronald saw what appeared to be a model of the invention, along with a good deal of other equipment scattered around that he didn't understand at all. Speaking with much enthusiasm, Mr. Desmond gave some explanations. Most of it was over Ronald's head, but he was able to gather that this was not just a battery, as he had been led to believe, but involved a modification of the ignition system.

"What did Mr. Bogus think about it?" asked Knight.

Mr. Desmond shot a quick glance at his son. "He agreed that I was working on an important new principle. The system works, make no mistake about that. But it's too bulky, too expensive to manufacture, and too erratic in operation. It would take a considerable amount of research in more suitable materials and better engineering design before the battery becomes practical. He estimated that he'd have to set up a million-dollar laboratory to try to get the bugs out of it, and those estimates have a way of turning out to be two or three times too low."

"Is he going to do it?" Knight demanded.

Mr. Desmond carefully picked up the lamp and led the way back into the cabin, closing the door after them. "I'm sorry, son, but he felt it was just too big a gamble."

"You mean he didn't want to take a chance on a man with your prison record?" said Knight harshly.

"He didn't say so, but it's quite possible that is what he was thinking. A huge contract like this would have to be justified to his board of directors."

"Wasn't he worried that one of his competitors might get ahead of him?" Ronald questioned. "Or to put it another way, is there anything to stop you from going to one of his competitors?"

"I seriously doubt that it would be any use. Are you familiar with the patent pool arrangement in the motor industry? What it amounts to is that the manufacturers all use each other's patents. You understand the reason for it. One manufacturer may have an excellent carburetor, another an excellent crankshaft, and so on, but unless they pooled their patents it would be impossible for a customer to buy a car that had a good *everything*. Nevertheless, the system does have its drawbacks, one of them being that the corporations are less willing to invest large sums in basic research, from which their competitors could share the results."

"So you've lost out on a million-dollar contract because of a cheap little three-hundred-dollar robbery," said Knight sourly.

His father cast another quick glance at him. "No, Larry, I didn't go to prison for a three-hundred-dollar robbery. If that had been all, I would certainly have had my sentence suspended. I went to prison because there was something else in my past, that early youthful error I'd made. I've never quite told you about it, and I won't now, except to say that I had been running around with a gang that was rather wild. Although I didn't do anything wrong myself, I tagged along with the others. I know that's not a good defense, either morally or legally, and I have no complaint to make about the sentence I served in the reformatory—if it could only have ended there. But it didn't end, and when something new came up, I was actually being punished once more for my earlier offense. That is why I would do almost anything I could to prevent a young person from making a mistake that might overshadow his whole future."

Knight turned upon Ronald suddenly. "All right, Wilford, you've got a pretty good idea how the whole affair went. I'll put it up to you straight: Who stole that money from the cash register?"

Ronald allowed his glance to move from son to father, and then slowly back to the son again. "I think I've known for quite some time, Knight. If your father didn't take the money, and you've convinced me he didn't, then there was only one other person who could have done it—yourself."

"You hit it squarely that time, Wilford," said Knight savagely. "Let me congratulate you. Yes, I stole the money, and my father went to prison to protect me. Not only that, but he deliberately stayed there six years so that the law could never touch me afterward. Six years, and all that time I could have perhaps saved him by opening my mouth. I didn't do it but eased my conscience by telling myself he could get out any time he wanted to by applying for a parole. That's your story for you, Wilford, one that Uglancie and Lister would give their eyeteeth to get. It's a swell feature, ought to make the front page, might even give you the byline you want. What kind of guy did you think I was, and what kind of guy do you think I am now?"

His father interrupted quietly, "I don't think it matters what Mr. Wilford thinks, Larry. The only thing of importance is what you think of yourself."

"Yes, but what am I supposed to think? There's more to this story yet, Wilford. Better get out your pencil and take some notes, for you'll want to be sure to get it straight... Because my mother died when I was very young, I was brought up by my dad. He did his best to give me a good home and upbringing, in fact gave me everything I needed and nearly everything I wanted. And how did I respond to this? I became spoiled and arrogant and thought if the world didn't give me what I wanted, I'd simply take it.

"I was a violin player of some promise, worked hard at it, and saw the possibility of a career in music. As I neared graduation, I received an offer from a musical conservatory for a partial scholarship. Unfortunately, my father wasn't able to provide the rest of the funds I would need, and I felt that an opportunity like this would never come to me again.

"So to get the money I needed, I simply helped myself from the cash register at the service station. I didn't actually plan the robbery, but when the chance came, I took advantage of it. Of course, I didn't intend that my father should be suspected of the robbery. I thought I could come back later in the evening, set off the burglar alarm, and escape. The trouble was that breaking the window would not set off the alarm. It aroused the people in the house next door who turned on a light and came to their front door to look out. I was scared, and high-tailed it for home, leaving the alarm still in operation, and sufficient evidence to send my father to prison. How about that, Dad? You knew all about it, didn't you?"

"Yes, I knew," his father replied. "It couldn't have been anyone else. Besides, I heard you going out that night."

"Now, Wilford, comes the worst part of my miserable story—how I let my father go to trial for the crime, constantly trying to convince myself that my testimony wasn't needed, and that my father would be acquitted without it. The verdict of guilty was a terrible shock, but even then I didn't speak up. I made excuses for myself—or rather, allowed other people to make excuses for me. I allowed myself to be persuaded there was nothing I could do for my father, and that he would be out in nine months for good behavior. Those nine months turned into six long, terrible, wasted years—years in which I was too ashamed even to write or visit him!"

"You mustn't worry about those six lost years, Larry," Mr. Desmond reassured him. "I was able to continue my work, and my studies, and even made some new friendships. The thing I most regretted, however, was that I didn't have the chance to be a father to you while you were growing up."

"Thanks, Dad," Barry answered, the intense bitterness still ringing through his voice, "for trying to help soothe my conscience, but it's not as simple as that. Actually I've done only one thing of which I am proud. When you left prison, I was shocked that you didn't look me up and apparently wanted nothing to do with me. I decided then I would find you, and if it seemed best for you to let the story be forgotten, I would do so. But if your vindication required making the story public, I would write it up—and that was the reason, Wilford, why I didn't know whether I could ever go back to the newspaper or not.

"But even then I found that the decision was no longer mine. There was Freddie Uglancie, waiting to use anything that might discredit me, and there was Mr. Bogus, who was negotiating for the invention. Dad made me promise I would do nothing until Mr. Bogus had made up his mind; but I had already determined that if my father lost this contract because of me, there was nothing in the world that could make me be silent any longer. That is still my decision, Dad. You know I'm right, don't you?"

Mr. Knight looked proud as he answered, "What I did was for a boy, Larry, but now you're a man and have to make a man's decisions."

He turned to Ronald with an eager look. "I'm glad to see that you haven't been taking any notes, Mr. Wilford, for I've a different version of this story to give you. I was a dreamer who thought only of an indefinite someday when my invention would bring me wealth and success and make my son proud of me. I forgot that my son was growing up day by day and needed my attention and companionship and a better living than I provided. He has said that I gave him nearly everything he needed or wanted, but that was only because he asked so little of me.

"Then, too, I encouraged him in his hopes of a career with the violin because his mother had been musical, and I wanted Larry to carry on. I don't really know whether he had talent enough for a career or not, but just the same I helped him to construct this dream castle until it became the most important thing in his life. Then, when his opportunity came, I was unable to help him take advantage of it. I think I've made it clear to you how much of the blame was really mine.

"My boy told you that he was selfish and arrogant. Let me tell you that heartsick over what he had done, he returned the money he had stolen without a word from anyone, only hoping that what he had done could be undone. He was unable to speak up for me at my trial because I planned it that way. I lied to him then, just as I lied to him later about being home in nine months, and how it would be useless for him to try to do anything for me.

"And let me say finally for my son, that I knew him for what he was, a fine, sturdy, intelligent boy, who has given me only one moment of doubt, but never in his life gave me one moment of shame. But let me conclude, that if I have felt pride in my son, there has never been a time when I felt as much pride in him as I do at this moment."

After a short silence during which Knight and his father looked at each other with deep understanding, Knight turned back to Ronald. "Well, there's your story, Wilford. Which way are you going to print it?"

Ronald looked at them both carefully, a smile touching his lips. "My assignment was to find Barry Knight, and I believe I can now wire back to the office: 'Mission accomplished.' I don't see any story here for me. It's your story now, Knight, and you'll have to tell it the way you think best."

CHAPTER 21

The Sound of Distant Thunder

Late Friday afternoon, Ronald, Ted, and their excess baggage in the form of Mr. Knight were on the bus headed back toward Union City. The snow sled had finally come through that morning, and Ronald and Ted remained in the village, sending up to the lodge for their suitcases since they did not desire another meeting with Lister and Grossen.

Barry Knight and his father had also come down on the snow sled, but had left town almost immediately in a hired car.

"First time I ever knew a reporter to give up a good story," Ted remarked to his brother, rather teasingly, for there was a certain amount of professional rivalry between them.

"Oh, I wouldn't say I gave up a story, Ted. I merely turned it over to a person who was much better qualified to write it than I was. The story's going to be in the paper next Monday. Knight called the newspaper this morning, and when I talked to Carole later, she told me what had been decided."

"I wonder, Ron—do you really think there's any point in publishing this story at all? It happened a long time ago—past the legal limit, so why not past the public limit as well?"

"That was Burnett's first reaction when Knight explained the matter to him, but Knight convinced him the story had to go in. It isn't simply a matter of clearing Mr. Desmond's reputation, but it's also to protect Knight's future reputation as well."

"I explained that to Ted already," Mr. Knight put in. "Knight can't go on living with a ghost."

"That's right. We don't know how much of this story Lister knows, but from what you've told me, I feel pretty sure he knows enough to print some sort of story about Knight. Even if he didn't, even if he doesn't have enough to go on, how could Knight ever be sure what he might discover and publish in the future? Knight's got too fine a future to endanger it in that way. Oh, incidentally, Carole told me that Knight offered his resignation, and Burnett told him to stop talking foolishness at long-distance rates, and to get on the job as fast as he could. Burnett can be pretty brusque when he wants to be."

"But just what sort of story is Knight going to write?" Ted wondered.

"Oh, I think he'll try to tell it just as truthfully as he can. But while he writes, he's going to have a sympathetic father peering pretty closely over his shoulder, and you can be sure Burnett will go over the story carefully before it's published to make certain Knight isn't too harsh on himself."

"You think the public will accept the story that way?"

"Well, how did *we* accept it? We saw a boy who wanted something so badly that he gave way to a moment of temptation. Believing he could make it look like an outside burglary, he had no expectation that his father would be implicated. Later he restored the money, would certainly have confessed in open court if his father hadn't prevented it, and even afterward would have told if his father hadn't convinced him it wouldn't do any good. It's the sort of youthful mistake we could easily forgive, and I think the public will accept it in that light. The only flaw in this thing is Lister. Even though he doesn't have the whole story, he may rush into print with something or other, and so much can depend on which story reaches the public first. If Lister's story comes first, it will seem as though Barry only wrote his story in an attempt to whitewash himself. But if Barry's story comes first, Lister's story will sound like sour grapes."

Ronald turned to Mr. Knight. "There's one detail that puzzles me. I didn't think Uglancie knew anything about Imperial, yet apparently he did. How did that happen?"

"Why, you told him yourself, Wilford."

"I did?" asked Ronald in surprise.

"Yes. You may not be aware of it, but Uglancie has a good many men stationed at strategic places throughout the state. He has supplied them with a list of license numbers they should always be on the alert for, and it should be flattering to you that your license number is among them. One of his men picked up your car going into Imperial, and by talking to the gas-station operator after you did, they had a line on Walter Desmond, which brought his name into the case. They still didn't know for sure that Barry Knight had ever lived in Imperial, but they figured you didn't know, either, and that maybe they could make up a story that would fool you. It was Uglancie's story, but—" he added with pride "—a good many of the details were my own invention."

"You think Mr. Bogus will accept Mr. Desmond's invention after all?" Ted asked of Ronald.

"That's hard to say. If Desmond's prison record is the only thing standing in the way, that will be speedily cleared up. But we can't be sure that was the real reason for the company's hesitation. Mr. Desmond says if he has a product they're interested in they'll buy it, but if he hasn't, then it was just a grand try that never quite came off."

"Funny thing," Ted went on, "here all the time everything made it look like Mr. Desmond was guilty, and none of us could really believe that an innocent man was sent to prison, and yet that was just what happened this time."

"No, Ted, I don't think I can go along with you there. I spoke with an authority at the penitentiary about that, and I don't think Mr. Desmond would fall within the category of an innocent man. Remember that he knew who did it, and was covering up for him, so regardless of how noble his action may have been, he didn't give the forces of the law a proper chance to fulfill their function."

The bus driver partly turned in his seat to call back to them. "Hear that?" They all listened and thought they heard a little rumbling in the distance. "That professor guy is dynamiting that other hill at the mouth of Lonely Valley, and I understand Hank Hudson is pretty huffy about it."

"I didn't know they were going to dynamite again," Ronald returned. "Was there a notice posted?"

"Oh, yes, it was posted in the post office and the inn. I thought everybody knew about it." He turned his attention back to the driving.

"I—er—wanted to tell you about that, Wilford," said Mr. Knight. "I wouldn't worry very much about anything Lister is going to do in the next couple of days. Some little hint that I dropped to him must have given him the wrong impression. He thought that Mr. Bogus was planning to meet you up in Lonely Valley the other night, but couldn't make it because of the dynamiting. So somehow he got the notion that there was another meeting planned for tonight, and he and Grossen are up at the cabin waiting for everybody." He chuckled. "I imagine they'll have as much trouble getting out of there as you did."

"Wasn't there a notice posted at the lodge?" Ronald questioned.

"Oh, yes, it was on the bulletin board, all right. But you know, I just happened to have a big calendar, and somehow it seemed to me that the bulletin board was the ideal place to hang it. Unfortunately it covered up most of the notices, but Hank didn't think to take it down until after Lister had left."

Ronald received this news with a grin and a nod of appreciation for Mr. Knight's talents as an actor.

"Well, this is Friday, Ted," he said later, stretching out his legs, "and I don't see any sense in trying to get back to the paper before Monday morning, so I think I'll just go along home with you and spend a day or two with Mom. Would you care to come along with us, Mr. Knight? Please excuse the name, but you've never given us any other."

"No, thank you, Wilford. I've grown rather attached to you and your brother, especially after that big lug tried twisting his arm—"

"What's that?" demanded Ronald, coming to attention. "Did Grossen do that to you? Why didn't you tell me?"

"Because it wasn't that important, and I didn't want anything to happen that might make you forget the newspaper story came first."

"Well, O.K., Ted, I'll drop it for now, but Marty Grossen better not ever cross my path again or there's likely to be fireworks. How'd you enjoy the skiing for the last couple of days, Ted?"

"It wasn't very good, but I guess I got enough of it to last me till next winter. As long as you were enjoying yourself so much up at Lonely Valley, I had to find something to do, and I didn't want to sit around looking at Lister and Grossen all day. I did do some work on those newspaper stories, though—the ones you promised to help me with."

"Well, which one did you decide to feature?"

"There's several pretty good ones, but that one by Margaret Lake—"

"There's no doubt that's the best."

"You never read it, but it really is pretty good—"

"Su-ure."

Mr. Knight interrupted grandly, "As I was saying, much as I appreciate your kind invitation, I find myself unable to accept the hospitality of your home. Fresh air may be all right in its place, but there's such a thing as overdoing it. Besides, at this time of year there's usually a fresh breeze right off the lake that comes swishing down Vincent Street and sweeps out some of the dust. Much as I've enjoyed this little vacation at our friend Mr. Uglancie's expense, I wouldn't want to be away from Short Vincent very long. There's too much I might miss."

"I don't know whether I've ever said much to you about Short Vincent, Ted," Ronald said to his younger brother. "It's a kind of legendary place that I'll have to visit to see for myself. The only thing that's stopping me is that I need a by-line first."

"I don't get it, Ron," said Ted frankly. "Why do you need a by-line before you can visit Short Vincent?"

"It's a long story, Ted. Remind me to tell you sometime."

THE TED WILFORD SERIES

1. *The Secret of Thunder Mountain* (1951)
2. *The Locked Safe Mystery* (1954)
3. *The Star Reporter Mystery* (1955)
4. *The Singing Trees Mystery* (1956)
5. *The Empty House Mystery* (1957)
6. *The Counterfeit Mystery* (1958)
7. *The Stolen Plans Mystery* (1959)
8. *The Scarecrow Mystery* (1960)
9. *The Big Cat Mystery* (1961)
10. *The Missing Witness Mystery* (1962)
11. *The Baseball Mystery* (1963)
12. *The Mystery of Rainbow Gulch* (1964)
13. *The Abandoned Mine Mystery* (1965)
14. *The S. S. Shamrock Mystery* (1966)
15. *The Greenhouse Mystery* (1967)